VISSER

Flip the pages to find out
what *really* happens
at the Yeerk Pool. . . .

Also by K.A. Applegate:

The EverWorld series

The Animorphs series

The Hork-Bajir Chronicles

The Andalite Chronicles

VISSER

K.A. APPLEGATE

SCHOLASTIC INC./New York

Library of Congress Cataloging-in-Publication Data

Applegate, K.A.
Visser / K.A. Applegate.
p. cm.
Companion book to: The Hork-Bajir chronicles.
Summary: On trial for treason, Edriss 562 explains how she infested a series of human hosts in order to spearhead the invasion of Earth by her people, the ruthless, parasitic Yeerks.

ISBN 0-439-08764-3

[1. Science fiction.] I. Title.
PZ7.A6483Vi 1999
[Fic] — dc21 99-31359
CIP
AC

12 11 10 9 8 7 6 5 4 3 2 1 9/9 0 1 2 3 4/0

Printed in the U.S.A.

First Scholastic printing, November 1999

Dedicated to Maxx Leach and all the students at Roosevelt School in Lubbock, Texas.

And to Michael and Jake

VISSER

PROLOGUE

"Honey?"

No answer. My husband was watching a game on television. He was preoccupied.

"Honey?" I repeated, adding more urgency to my tone of voice.

He looked over. Smiled sheepishly. "What's up?"

"Marco's fever is down. I think he's basically over this thing. He's asleep. Anyway, I was thinking of getting some fresh air."

He muted the television. "Good idea. It's tough when they're sick, huh? Kids. He's okay, though, huh?"

"It's just a virus."

"Yeah, well, take some time, you've been carrying the load. And if you're going to the store —"

"Actually, I think I'll go down to the marina."

He laughed and shook his head. "Ever since you bought that boat . . . I think Marco has some competition as the favorite child in this household." He frowned. "You're not taking it out, are you? Looks kind of gloomy out."

I made a smile. "Just want to make sure it's well secured, check the ropes and all."

He was back with the game. He winced at some error made by his preferred team. "Uh-huh. Okay."

I stepped back, turned, and walked down the hall. The door to Marco's room was ajar. I paused to look inside. I almost couldn't do otherwise because the other voice in my head, the beaten-down, repressed human voice, was alive and screaming and screaming at me, begging me, pleading <No! No! No!>

Marco was still asleep. Or pretending to be. A good-looking kid, but small. Already, in his early adolescence, the stamp of failure was on him. He was too sweet-natured and trusting ever to make it very far in a hard world. A world that would only grow harder for humans.

Much harder, if I had my way.

I looked at him, one last time, as the voice in my head kept begging and begging. <Let me at least say good-bye, let me hold him one last time, let me kiss him, oh my God, no, no, don't do this!>

But that was only a voice. The voice of someone who no longer had a say in what I did with this body, this life.

I left the house. I drove the car to the marina.

The wind was coming up. Earth really does have fascinating weather. So many different permutations. Blazing heat and brain-numbing cold; storms that bring violent winds or driving snows or rains so heavy they blot out all light.

I climbed out of the car and sauntered jauntily along to the boat, a small sailboat tied up halfway down the pier. Much bigger boats were tied up on either side. That was okay. I had all the boat I needed.

I climbed aboard and cast off the lines. I winched up the mainsail and took the tiller. I didn't use the engine, not even for getting out of the marina. Anyone could guide a powerboat. It took skill to sail.

Sailing was one of the best things about being in a human. It was such a perfect blend of power and subtlety, bending to the inevitable and yet resisting great forces. Dangerous and exhilarating. You skimmed along between sea and sky, a part of each, trusting neither.

I raised more sail than was prudent and stood out toward the open sea. I would be seen sailing. And seen to be carrying too much sail. That was important. Humans need someone to blame for every mishap. There is no room for random chance in the limited human cosmology. So I was providing them with the culprit: Me.

"She went out in bad weather," they would say.

"Carried too much sail. Amateur sailor. Weekend sailor. No respect for the sea." That's what they would say, and they'd blame the victim and move on.

In an hour or so, once I was out of sight of land, I would lower my sails and wait for a Bug fighter to come lift me off the deck. The engine backwash of the Bug fighter would capsize the boat. Or I might put the Taxxon pilot to the test and see if he could ram the low-slung boat. That would puzzle the humans.

Either way, my body would never be found.

The husband, the son who belonged to the voice inside my head, they would think I had died.

The human woman named Eva, the husk, the human shell I lived in, would cease to exist as far as any human knew. I would be given the inevitable superstitious send-off. A ceremony, but there'd be no body to put in the grave.

Eva's human mind would still be with me, of course. Still blubbering and weeping and begging, no doubt. But I had written the book on human infestation. I would have no difficulty controlling this woman.

I understood her, this mother-human. Understood her in ways neither she, nor anyone else, would ever be allowed to know.

The family had served me well, for a time, as I

completed my knowledge of humans. But now I would have greater duties. Duties that would take me far from the dull life I'd accepted as a way to learn about our next conquest.

My time of lying low was over. The notice had at last come: I was promoted, leaping over so many desperately ambitious competitors to take the most powerful position short of membership on the Council of Thirteen.

I would spearhead the invasion of Earth. I would take charge of our greatest conquest. I would stand alone atop the Yeerk military hierarchy.

I was to become Visser One.

CHAPTER 1

VISSER ONE

"Honored members of the Council of Thirteen, I am present at this trial under protest. I do not deny your right to hold me for trial. You are entitled to know anything and everything about my loyal service to the Empire. But that my inquisitor should be none other than my most relentless enemy, himself a traitor, is intolerable!"

I spoke to the holographic representation of the Council. Thirteen Yeerks in various host bodies: Nine Hork-Bajir, two Taxxons, and two whose bodies were so concealed that I could not guess at their form.

They were dressed in dark red robes, so dark they were almost black. They stood, motionless, held in place, suspended by gravity-neutral fields, fed by a continuous refined current of Kandrona rays.

The Hork-Bajir-Controllers wore a lightweight

mesh beneath their robes to keep the wrist and arm blades from slicing through the robe's fabric.

The two Taxxon-Controllers were bloated, monstrously inflated versions of the great centipedes. Both were attended by Gedds, ready with freshly killed meat to feed the eternal hunger that not even a Yeerk inside that feverish brain can control. Their ceremonial robes were as large as sails, wrapped around the raised front third of their bodies.

They were light-years away, of course. They would see me, my host face and body in three dimensions. They could also watch my vital signs, translated into universal equivalents. Blood pressure, heart rate, hormone production, all reduced to digital readouts a billion miles away. And they could, with a thought, call up whatever data had been compiled on specific events or locations or individuals.

They could also hear and see my inquisitor. They would hear his thought-speak voice — his host body's normal mode of communication. His host body was the envy of the Yeerk Empire. For he alone, of all Yeerks, possessed an Andalite host.

He rested comfortably on four almost dainty hooves. His body was standard quadruped grazer: like an Earth deer or horse, or a *Desbadeen limner.*

He had an upper body similar to many species, but most similar, perhaps, to that of a human, with the symmetrical shoulders and hanging arms ending in multi-digit hands.

The face was mouthless, an Andalite oddity. Andalites eat by crushing and absorbing grasses through their hooves as they run. They communicate mind-to-mind.

There were three things that made the Andalites inherently formidable as enemies: their agile intelligence, their ability to shape thought-speak to either wide-band or private communication, and, of course, their faster-than-the-eye-can-see tails.

Many a careless Yeerk has died from the blade of an Andalite tail.

Beyond their impressive physical makeup there is the matter of Andalite technology. Specifically the morphing technology that allows them to absorb DNA from any animal source and then painlessly, and almost effortlessly, become that animal.

Visser Three remained silent as I complained. He was a fool, but not so great a fool that he would provoke the Council by trying to cut me off.

His eyes wore an alien smirk. He waited patiently. He had already won. I was his prisoner. This was his great moment.

"You will have plenty of time to make statements, Visser One," a Council member said. I did not know who.

Visser Three, straining to sound obsequious,

said, <I would remind the Council that this creature has already been demoted. She no longer holds the rank of Visser One.>

"That was a temporary reduction in rank. This trial will determine whether that reduction is permanent. Or whether, indeed, Visser One is allowed to live. For now she will be referred to by her formal rank."

Garoff? Was it Garoff speaking for the Council? I couldn't tell. Nor could I be sure whether it was good news or bad that my mentor would be taking a leading role.

"Computer: the charges."

In the Council's chamber the computer read the charges against me. "The Yeerk, Edriss-Five-Six-Two, holding the rank of Visser One is charged with the following crimes: treason by incompetence, which carries a sentence of death by Dracon beam; treason by violation of established procedure, which carries a sentence of death by Dracon beam; treason by sympathy with a subject species, which carries a sentence of death by Kandrona starvation; treason by contact with the foul Andalite race, which carries a sentence of death by torture; treason by murder of subordinate Yeerks, which carries a sentence of exile to punishment duty."

Five charges of treason. Four death sentences. My greatest fear was death by Kandrona starvation.

And it was my most likely prospect. Unless I could outwit Visser Three.

<Now. Tell us your version of events,> Visser Three said.

"I'll tell the *truth*," I snapped.

<The Council will judge the truth or falsity of your statements. You've heard the charges. Do you acknowledge, deny, or, claim mitigation?>

"I deny. The charges are lies. Not only lies, but unintelligent lies. Typical of you, Visser Three."

He smirked, patient, in no hurry, enjoying this beyond measure. His large main eyes — Andalite eyes — watched me. The two stalk eyes roamed here and there, checking the equipment, watching the ceremonial thirteen Hork-Bajir guards that stood at attention around our small, secure room.

I knew that even now Visser Three felt a measure of fear. But not of me. We were on Earth, and Earth has not been kind to Visser Three. A small guerilla band has bedeviled his efforts to follow through on the great conquest begun by me. Visser Three believes these guerillas to be Andalite survivors of their destroyed Dome ship.

I know differently. Yes, the group no doubt contains one or more Andalites. But it also contains humans. Humans who have, somehow, acquired morphing technology.

<It will be for the Council of Thirteen, wise leaders

of the far-flung Yeerk Empire, to decide whether the accusations are true or false,> Visser Three said, sanctimony in every syllable. Then, in private thought-speak that only I could hear, he added, <And when they convict you it will be I who administers the punishment. It will take a long time for you to die, Visser One. I can make a Kandrona starvation last weeks.>

I showed nothing on my human face. I was no longer able to show much emotion on my human face. The left side of my head was burned almost beyond recognition, red and black and raw. My mouth was twisted from blows delivered while imprisoned.

I had been badly injured in a fall. A final, terrible battle between Visser Three and me. A battle that had been engineered, I later realized, by the so-called Andalite bandits, in a rather clever and ambitious attempt to have Visser Three and I kill each other.

The Visser's threat was real. I knew that if the Council found against me, Visser Three would keep me in agony until I lost my sanity. But it could not be much worse than the last month of captivity. My broken bones, right leg, left arm and shoulder, ribs, and my burned flesh had been left untreated. All could be easily repaired. None had been.

I could not cut myself off entirely from the pain

my host felt. Not without releasing my host altogether. She felt the pain, and so did I. But she did not share the deepest pain: Visser Three had kept me on the edge of Kandrona starvation. I was weak. Wracked with pain. Already in the bare, early stages of Kandrona starvation. *Only* a Yeerk can know that feeling.

My host, the human, Eva, had been emboldened by my weakness. I no longer had the strength to silence her voice inside my head. She taunted me. Distracted me. She hates me, of course.

<Soon he'll kill you,> she said. <Soon evil will destroy evil.>

<The pain may well be yours as much as mine,> I told her.

<No, no, it won't,> she said. <Because for you it will be defeat. For me it will be liberation.>

I tried to ignore the voice. I had greater problems than a jeering host.

<Begin,> Visser Three said. <You may tell your tale in any order you choose. This is *your* defense. There are no limits except for one: You must end within one feeding cycle. You have three days.>

Liar. He knew I was within half a day of needing Kandrona rays. But he would not defeat me. No, not even now. I would tell my tale. Most of it.

I looked into the hologram, looked at each member of the Council in turn. And I began.

CHAPTER 2

My name is Edriss-Five-Six-Two, of the Sulp Niar pool.

I will begin this story at a time in my career when I controlled a Hork-Bajir host body and held the rank of Sub-Visser Four-hundred-nine. My area of specialization was intelligence. Current assignment? Target acquisition.

I was part of a team that analyzed data from a wide variety of sources. Data that would, we hoped, lead us to what we all longed for so desperately: a Class-Five subject race.

I was young. Young to be a sub-visser, but already impatient to be more. And this job was surely not the path to greater things.

I was third in command at Olgin base, a dusty, irrelevant backwater of bare-bones buildings on the day–night line of a moon we'd actually purchased from the Skrit Na.

As the Council knows, the Skrit Na are useless as hosts, and not terribly threatening as foes. But there was no point in starting unprofitable wars, so rather than seize the base, we bought it. The price? A captured Andalite drone ship.

Cheap. And still we overpaid.

Olgin base was good for only one thing: Its Zero-space transit point made it convenient for quick data transmission from the widespread elements of the fleet, and from our two main planets: the Taxxon home world, and the Hork-Bajir home world.

Our own planet was then, as now, surrounded by orbiting Andalite warships. The day would come when we would retake our world and the pools that spawned us. But not yet. The Andalites were still too strong for us to risk a head-to-head, all-out conflict.

Before we could face the Andalites we needed a more numerous, more agile, more adaptable host. Gedds were clumsy and weak, with senses that were distorting and unreliable. The Taxxons were allies more than true hosts, and in any event, not even the most strong-willed Yeerk could control the insane, cannibalistic hunger of a Taxxon.

The Hork-Bajir had done well for us. They were naturally strong and dangerous. Clumsy for detail work, but the other strengths compensated.

As the Council knows, the problem with the Hork-Bajir was that there simply weren't enough of them. The Andalites, those moral paragons, had

exterminated most of the Hork-Bajir race rather than let it fall into our hands.

We *had* thousands of Hork-Bajir. We *needed* millions of hosts. My task — which seemed futile at the time — was to find those hosts.

Anyone at Olgin base with the slightest influence, the most tenuous connection to a highly placed officer, managed to get reassigned. Yeerks were leaving all the time. And replacements, poor, unwanted trash for the most part, were being sent to us.

One of my duties was to indoctrinate the new recruits. I started as they de-shipped. The ship berths were not a pleasant environment. Cargo was constantly in motion, by puller and pusher, by strap, and even carried on the backs of Gedds.

"There are five classes of alien," I said, eyeing the dozen Gedds, Hork-Bajir, and Taxxons lined up before me. "Who can name the five?"

Several started to answer, but I held up my hand, indicating they should remain silent.

"I should say . . . who can name them if I mention that the mangling of a single word, or the misstatement of a single fact will result in your being fed to Taxxons?"

This was my little joke, of course. It is nearly impossible to get a coherent sentence out of a Gedd mouth. And flatly impossible with a Taxxon who can, at best, hiss and sputter in its own language. Meaning no disrespect to the Council members who hold Taxxon hosts.

Hork-Bajir are the best communicators, of course, despite their brains' innate quirk of confusing various languages.

No one laughed at my joke. Good. They were beginning to understand: I was the boss. They were mine to dispose of as I saw fit.

"There are five classes of alien," I continued. "Class One: those physically unfit for infestation — the Skrit Na being a good example because of their annoying need to phase. Class Two: those who can be infested but that suffer from serious physical drawbacks — such as the Taxxons and our own Gedds. Class Three: those that can be infested, suffer from no physical debility, but exist in only small numbers and cannot be quickly bred." I used my hand to indicate my own Hork-Bajir body.

"Four: those that would be excellent targets for infestation but that are, for now at least, too formidable to challenge. Can anyone name an example?"

Dead silence. They all knew the example, of course. But they were afraid that saying it out loud might constitute treason.

"Oh, come, come now," I prodded. "We all know who we mean: our former mentors and present-day tormentors, the Andalites."

Nervous glances. Like maybe I'd crossed the line myself.

"And then, there are Class-Five aliens: Aliens who are right for infestation, exist in large numbers, and do not have the power to resist us. That, my fellow Yeerks, is our mission here. To find the real, live example of Class Five."

"If theyrrrr even rrrr-exist." It was one of the Gedds.

I stepped close. "Your name?"

"Rrr-Kilgam-Thrrrrree Rrr-Two-Nine."

Quick as lightning I struck. My wrist blade swept up and across. The Gedd's throat gushed blue blood. The body collapsed instantly. He clutched feebly at his throat.

I was glad it was a Gedd. If it had been a Hork-Bajir I couldn't have wasted the host body, even as a lesson.

Kilgam-Three-Two-Nine tried to crawl out of the Gedd's ear. He made it halfway before the host body died.

They say it's very, very difficult to get out of a dead host before death reaches you as well. Very difficult.

I reached down and with my sharp Hork-Bajir

claws I widened the ear canal. I picked up Kilgam and handed him to one of the Hork-Bajir.

"Better take him to the pool," I said.

"But . . . But, Sub-Visser, I . . . I don't know where it is, we just arrived at this base!"

So I led the way to the pool. I had made my point: Their lives were mine, never mind the new regulations against killing subordinates. If they displeased me, they would die, law or no law. But I was not unreasonable. As I had the power to kill, so I had the power to give life.

That's the subtlety so many Yeerks miss. Threats are very useful. But for the more subtle, and thus complete control over your subordinates, you need the helping hand as well as the killing blade.

I had given the same speech, the same demonstration of seriousness a dozen times. I'd never failed to instill a sense of duty in my charges.

And yet, it was all pointless. We were searching for something that might not exist. And something that, in any event, would not be found by we poor, abandoned nonentities on a base the Empire had forgotten.

I was feeling rather self-pitying as I led this latest collection of half-wits to the pool, when I was interrupted by a rushing Hork-Bajir. It was my adjutant, Methit-Five-Seven-Two.

"Sub-Visser! Sub-Visser!"

"Yes, Methit?"

"A report. Just in. One of our people, a sub-visser stationed on the Taxxon planet, has just forwarded a report of a new species." Methit caught his breath.

"And?" I prodded.

"And he claims . . . the report is, that it's Class Five."

I felt my Hork-Bajir hearts jump. "Probably a false alarm," I said blandly. "What is this species called?"

"Humans, Sub-Visser. They are called humans. And . . . and the report claims that they may exist in large numbers. Not millions. Billions."

CHAPTER 3

That report came from the Yeerk who would later rise to the rank of Visser Three.

Of course back then he was a lowly sub-visser, like myself. Higher on the ladder, certainly, but still a sub-visser.

I was very skeptical of the report at first. But then the holograph images began to arrive. Transmission speed was slower then. It took hours for the images to load up in the computer. I sat, staring, transfixed by pictures of two humans.

They were gender differentiated, like Andalites and Hork-Bajir. One was male. He gave his name as Chapman. The other was female. Named Loren.

They had been taken by the Skrit Na. Of course the Council is familiar with the habits of the Skrit Na. They are forever visiting planets, kidnapping local species, and performing inexplicable medical experiments on them, carrying them off only to return them later, and so on.

The Skrit Na, true to form, had seized these two humans for reasons known only to the Skrit Na.

A passing Andalite fleet evidently spotted the Skrit Na ship and decided to board it. We do not know why. Perhaps Visser Three knows why, but I do not.

In any event, the Andalites boarded the Skrit Na ship and found the two human captives. Then, again for reasons I do not know, this single Andalite scout ship headed for Taxxon space.

They may have been following a second Skrit Na ship. One did land at the Taxxon spaceport shortly before the Andalites arrived and seized one of our transport ships in orbit.

They used this transport ship to evade our defenses and land on the Taxxon planet. There were various events associated with that time, although the sequence is uncertain in the record.

What we do know is that at least one of the Andalites, and the two humans, were taken by Yeerk security forces. Taken, though not held for long.

Two humans, three Andalites. And not just any Andalites. The leader of the expedition was an Andalite War-Prince named Alloran-Semitur-Corrass. Alloran the criminal who released the Quantum virus into the Hork-Bajir home world and helped to deprive us of the full fruits of our just victory there.

*   *   *

The members of the Council murmured. They knew the name Alloran.

Of course they knew that name. There was only one Andalite-Controller. One Andalite host. Nevertheless, I drove the point home.

"Members of the Council will mark that name: Alloran. This is the Andalite who later became host to none other than Visser Three.

"And one other of the three Andalites in this party, though a mere cadet, also bore a name that will be remembered by Yeerks: Elfangor-Sirinial-Shamtul."

Another reaction, stronger this time. The name Elfangor was a curse word. No other single Andalite has done us more damage.

"Yes, honored members, it was Visser Three who, on that fateful occasion, came into contact with the mass-murderer Alloran and the criminal Elfangor.

"Ponder that fact. Keep that fact in mind as I continue with my story. Keep in mind that Visser Three, this very Yeerk who charges me with treason, met, communicated with and, I charge, befriended Alloran and Elfangor!"

The same Council member who had spoken be-

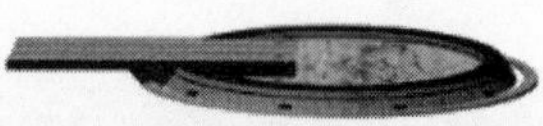

fore, stirred. "What are you implying, Visser One?" I could see now that it was, indeed, Garoff-One-Six-Eight.

"I imply nothing," I said. "I do not imply. I assert! I avow! I accuse, honored members, I accuse!" I pointed a finger at Visser Three. It's a wonderfully useful and dramatic human gesture. I stuck out my unbroken right arm and pointed a trembling finger at Visser Three.

"I accuse! There! There is your traitor!"

CHAPTER 4

<Silence!> Visser Three erupted. He leaped forward, whipped his Andalite tail up over his head, blade quivering, ready to strike, ready to slice my head from my shoulders.

"Are you so terrified of the truth, Visser?" I demanded.

<I killed Elfangor myself! I morphed and lifted him up and ate him!>

"You were eliminating a potential witness against you, Visser Three."

<I'll kill you now!>

It was perfect! The fool was unable to control himself and by his own wild panic had given credibility to my charges.

"Desist, Visser Three," a voice said. A Hork-Bajir voice. Again, it was Garoff-One-Six-Eight. The member responsible for counterintelligence. So. He would be speaking for the Council throughout my trial. Which meant his opinion would count for a very great deal.

Garoff also controlled the security troops ringing Visser Three and me. A word from him would send Hork-Bajir slashing into us.

Visser Three shook with the effort to control himself.

I smiled at him and whispered, "We shall see who is really on trial here, Visser."

"There will be no more disruption," Garoff said calmly. "Visser One, continue. But stick to your narrative. You are not to engage in conversation with Visser Three."

I bowed my head in submission. I had scored my points. I had planted suspicion of Visser Three in the minds of the Council.

And Visser Three knew it. The smug look was gone, wiped away. It was beginning to dawn on him that his own life was now at risk.

<Now who's the fool, Edriss?> my host, Eva, sneered. <They'll execute you both. You can't be saved, honey. They'll starve you, Edriss. And my son will live to dance on both your graves!>

<Your precious Marco won't survive this, that I promise you!> I threatened.

She laughed. She, better than anyone, knew my weakness. She, better than anyone, knew I'd die rather than hand Visser Three a victory over the "Andalite bandits."

I continued, speaking again to the Council.

Carefully projecting the calm of the innocent, in contrast to Visser Three.

In any event, Council members, I received this information of a new species. A possible Class-Five species. My assignment was to validate and evaluate the data.

Accordingly, I directed all our long-range technical capability toward the planet these humans called "Earth." Unfortunately, I did not have a precise location. The Skrit Na are excellent record keepers, and their ship's computer would have shown the precise location, however, somehow that ship was allowed to escape Taxxon space. That Skrit Na ship . . . in the custody of Visser Three . . . escaped.

No doubt a coincidence.

What I did have available was the Skrit Na's trajectory out of Z-space. That was data in our orbital and deep space sensors. I could extrapolate. I narrowed the location of Earth down to an area of approximately four-thousand systems.

It took a full year, eliminating system by system, those without planets, those with no planets that could support carbon-based life-forms, and so on. In the end I narrowed it down to three possible systems.

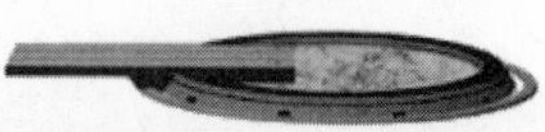

I reported this fact to my then superior, Sub-Visser Seventeen, the new base commander. I was told that I was wasting my time.

And I was told that I was to be transferred. My new post would be anti-insurgent work on the Taxxon home world. I would be given a new host body. A Taxxon.

A Taxxon. With all that implied for those not of very high rank. I nodded toward the two Taxxon Council members. The eternal hunger. The life in tunnels. The knowledge that any slight injury would be fatal, as I was set upon by other Taxxons, eaten alive!

I had discovered the location of a Class-Five species! And I was to be exiled to the Taxxon home world. It was insane! Insane!

I knew that something was wrong. Someone . . . *someone* . . . was working to keep the secret of Earth hidden. My supervisor, Sub-Visser Seventeen? Yes, of course. But at whose behest?

I rolled my eyes toward Visser Three and was rewarded by the sight of several Council members unconsciously following my lead, looking toward Visser Three. Of course I found out later that Visser Three had had nothing to do with the orders. They were mere stupidity, not conspiracy.

* * *

Members of the Council, I had a choice. I could follow my orders, consign myself to the Taxxon home world where my death could be easily arranged by the very person who had arranged my transfer . . . I could abandon the only Class-Five race known to exist . . . or, I could violate my orders and go in search of the species that could make us supreme throughout the galaxy.

It was no choice at all. As a loyal Yeerk, I had to defy my treasonous orders. And so I did.

I enlisted a subordinate, Essam-Two-Nine-Three, a fellow Hork-Bajir Controller, and took a scout ship and set off alone through Zero-space in search of Earth.

<You *stole* a ship!> Visser Three yelled. <By her own words she is convicted of a death penalty offense! Honored Council members, she has just forfeited her life! Let me take her now, right now. She has no right to live a moment longer!>

"Silence!" Garoff snapped. "The Council has long known about this, and has long since pardoned the offense."

Visser Three started to object, stopped himself, fell silent.

Garoff's black-red hood moved slowly, side to side. "Visser One, I believe you have previously recorded the incidents involved in this part of your story on memory dump?"

I nodded. "Yes, Council Member. I made a memory dump shortly after —"

"Then I suggest we all access the Memory Transfer Protocol. We can see the original, true memories that way. And without interruption."

<Yes, that would be best,> Visser Three jumped in. <The memory dump is the best, truest way to see events as they transpired.>

He paused just for a beat, then added, <It leaves us to wonder why Visser One has not chosen to make memory dumps of other, more recent events. What is she hiding?>

Garoff said, "Yeerks of Visser rank are not required to make memory dumps. That indignity is reserved for lower ranks."

"I will make a complete memory dump available," I said quickly. "The instant that Visser Three agrees to do the same."

A bluff, of course. Neither of us could afford a total memory dump. There are more than a hundred death penalty or exile offenses. In the course of acting as a loyal Yeerk Visser I had probably violated a third of them. And, of course, Visser Three had violated still more, beginning with summary execution of subordinates. Visser Three had slaughtered subordinates by the poolful.

And, of course, no Yeerk had risen to the Council without breaking the very laws they promulgated.

I locked eyes with my foe. We were two experienced, expert killers. Two leaders of Yeerks. Two generals.

Only one of us would survive this trial.

The Council accessed the Memory Transfer Protocol. Visser Three did the same. All of us would see what happened to me on that desperate mission, just as it happened. They would see it through my senses, my memories. Just as I saw it. Just as I felt it.

I accepted the patch that was applied to my head by a Taxxon technician. I would see the same memories as all the others.

But for me, the protocol was unnecessary. I remembered every detail.

Every detail.

CHAPTER 5

Stored Memory Transfer Protocol

Essam-293 turned to me, his eyes wary, concerned. "I have rechecked our supplies, Sub-Visser," he said. "My initial calculations were correct. We have enough food to keep our host bodies alive for only seven more days. Enough water for only three days. If one of us leaves his host and returns to the mini-pool, the other host body can survive for twice that time."

"If this is the right system all that computation will be moot," I said. "If this is not the correct system then yes, you will leave your host and return to the mini-pool."

"Yes, Sub-Visser."

"Don't worry so much, Essam. If we have to kill your host we'll soon find you a replacement."

He nodded his Hork-Bajir head. He knew I was lying. By now Essam had figured out that I was on an unauthorized mission. If things went badly he would be blamed, same as me. Even if things went well, he might not be given a new host anytime soon. None might be available.

And, of course, he had to consider the possibility that I would simply kill him to simplify my life and stretch my supplies.

But Essam was no fool. He knew better than to challenge me openly. I had chosen him carefully. He was a Yeerk of narrow expertise: a pilot and technician. He had at one point risen to the rank of sub-visser. But he had suffered demotion for an incident of poor judgment. While on patrol he had allowed a handful of Hork-Bajir to escape aboard a neutral *Desbadeen* ship.

A Yeerk who failed to understand that diplomatic niceties like "neutrality" were nonsense was unfit for command.

I had sensed this peculiar weakness in Essam, this confusion of purpose. This lack of serious ambition. That made him perfect for my purposes. I needed a competent servant, not a competitor.

We translated from Zero-space, popping suddenly out of the blank, white closeness of the place that is no place, into the blackness of real space.

"Congratulations, Essam. That was excellent navigation."

The yellow star was very close. Close enough to make you flinch. From my vantage point it could be

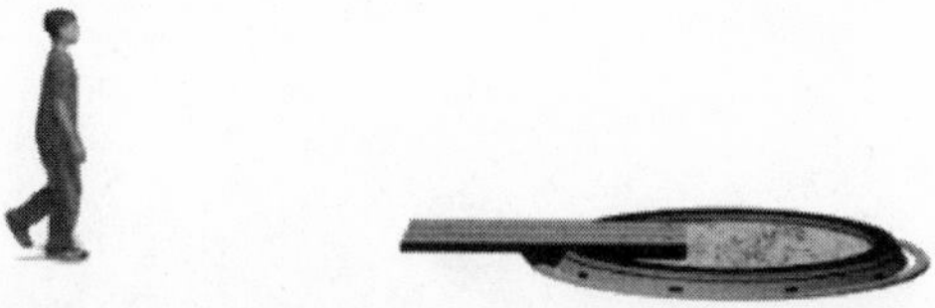

seen clearly as a seething mass of burning, churning, erupting gasses, not as the atmosphere-dimmed thing one sees from a planet surface.

I aimed the sensors away from the star. Out toward the planets. The sensors began to churn out raw data.

There were two medium-sized gas giants, one with an attractive set of rings. Both had a number of moons, some of which, at least, might sustain life.

Essam looked questioningly.

"No," I said. "We'll start with the planets. Moons later."

He was curious. "Is there a reason?"

I smiled. "Instinct. I have been searching for this species a very long time. I pictured them with a true planet. Not a moon."

Further out from the two big gas spheres were smaller gaseous planets. But in closer to the yellow star were four solid-form planets.

The one nearest the star was tiny, brutally hot, not a likely prospect. The next out, though larger, was nearly as hot, with terrific winds and pressures. It might sustain life, but not the soft-skinned things I'd seen in the holograms.

The third and fourth planets were clearly the most likely to be populated. One was the red of oxidized ferrous metal.

The other, the third planet, was blue.

My heart leaped. I knew. I knew.

And then the sensor data began to explode into the computers and onto the screens. The blue planet was spewing forth radio band signals, X-ray signals, microwave signals in a profusion that simply overwhelmed the computers. The ship's sensors were intercepting trillions of bits per second.

The blue planet was alive.

I put the ship into high orbit around planet number three. We needed time to prepare. I couldn't afford to just go blundering in, Dracon beams blasting. If I handled this first contact badly it could lose us this species for all time.

I needed to assess their strengths and weaknesses. I needed to know whether what we saw before us, this blue and green and brown sphere at the edge of nowhere was a true Class Five. Or whether, despite what I'd seen of the humans Loren and Chapman, we were dealing with a Class Four: another race, like the Andalites, too powerful for conquest.

At that moment, watching the raw-data totals, the unimaginable trillions of bits of electronic data swamping our computer, I was worried. How could any species generate this much data and not be formidable?

I began to draw off samples of the data. Much of it was incomprehensible. It appeared to be composed of auditory or visual tracks. Snatches of conversation:

"Hey, t'sup?"

"Nothin', man."

"Yeah. Same here. So, what did he say?"

"He was all, like, 'no problem.' And I was like 'uh, reality check, okay?'"

"No way!"

And a type of conversation that was accompanied by rhythmic sounds arranged in patterns.

And there was a more complex type of data that combined conversation with the rhythmic sounds and had a visual element as well. There were images of humans wearing body coverings, sitting close together while rhythmic sounds played, then stopped. Then the humans conversed.

"Welcome back to *Today.* In this half hour we'll be talking with our panel of military analysts about the latest developments in Operation Desert Storm. And, in our cooking segment . . ."

It was bewildering. Absurd. Insane. Too much, far, far too much. Why would there be a need for communications this frequent? The only necessary communications are orders from above, progress reports from below, and basic logistical matters. The entire Yeerk Empire did not generate a thousandth of this data.

"What's in orbit?" I asked Essam.

He interfaced with the computer. "Perhaps a hundred nonnatural objects, all apparently small, automated transmission or surveillance devices."

"No ships? No orbital weapons arrays?"

He rechecked the computer. "Sensors show several thousand atmospheric craft below, but none beyond the atmosphere. No evidence of orbital defenses. And there are very few sensors aimed outward from the planet. Those sensors are simple visible light or X-ray detectors."

"The moon?"

"I detect signs that humans have visited their moon, but no humans are currently on the moon." Essam shook his head disparagingly. "Feckless creatures, that much seems certain."

I began to experience renewed hope. No space-based weapons. No spacecraft at all, at least not at the moment. By contrast, the environs of the Andalite home world bristled with weapons and teemed with ships.

The humans were no Class-Four species.

"We'll never understand this species from up here," I said. "We have to land."

Essam hesitated. "Sub-Visser, you yourself said that we need data on these creatures."

"Yes. But we have too much data. Too much to know where to start. We need a human to act as translator."

"Is that wise, Sub-Visser?"

"Wise? Maybe not, Essam. But if those creatures down there are a Class-Five species I'll be a full Visser. If they are not, I'll be executed for disobeying an order. It's time to find out."

He started to say something, stopped himself.

"You worry too much, Essam. Those creatures down there? Those humans? They're mine, Essam. Mine!"

CHAPTER 6

Essam piloted the ship down. We detected primitive sensor arrays, what the humans call radar, but those were easily evaded.

We landed on the dark side of the planet. We had no knowledge of human physical capabilities. But the fact that they used artificial lighting made it logical that they were night-blind.

We headed for an empty area, an arid zone far from the large, bright clusters of human cities. The nearest major human habitation was more than a hundred miles away, to the northeast.

Down we went, down through the darkness of Earth's night. I felt my excitement building. It was a momentous occasion. A historic occasion. If I was right, if these were Class-Five aliens, my future was assured. I would be the most respected, and soon thereafter the most feared, Yeerk in the Empire.

Down, down, slipping through the primitive radar, slowing as the empty, barren land rose up to meet us.

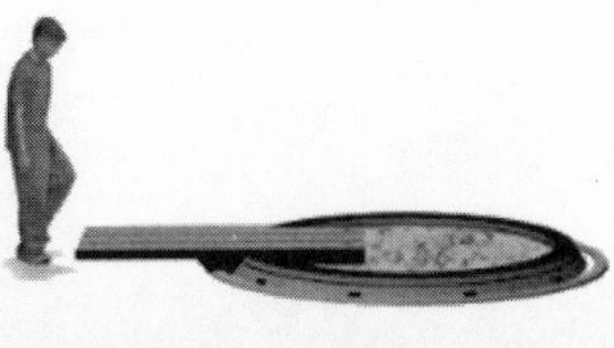

We landed. Essam looked at me, questioning.

"Atmosphere?" I asked.

"As the long-range sensors showed: nitrogen, carbon dioxide, oxygen, and various trace gases as well as particulates. Breathable for Hork-Bajir bodies. Though a bit more oxygen-rich than necessary."

I nodded. So much the better. A species that breathed methane would be of little use to us on the Hork-Bajir or Taxxon worlds. Let alone when we finally invaded the Andalite home world.

"Break out two Dracon weapons," I ordered. "The rules of engagement are simple: No human who sees us may escape alive. We will attempt to capture and infest one or two humans, as circumstances permit."

"Yes, Sub-Visser."

"Open the outer hatch."

The hatch opened. I got up, bent low, stuck my head and shoulders out into alien atmosphere. I breathed deep. The air seemed bitter-tasting and dry to my Hork-Bajir senses. But it was mine. All of it, mine. And that made it a perfect still-pool lagoon as far as I was concerned.

I descended the steps. I planted my Hork-Bajir foot on the sandy, almost powdery soil of Earth. I looked to my left and right.

The sky was black. The earth around me just as

black. The stars above cast insignificant illumination, and Earth's moon was below the horizon.

"Night vision," I ordered. Essam came down out of the ship, carrying the small spray vial. He aimed the aerosol at my eyes and sprayed. There was a tingle, then, within seconds, the night was brighter. Not so bright as day, but bright enough for me to see that we were not alone.

Perhaps a quarter mile away was a line of creatures, plainly visible with my enhanced night vision. They had large round heads, nearly as large as my own. The top half of the head was larger, like a shell placed over a smaller head beneath. They had two arms, both also quite large.

My first thought was that they looked like humans. The head, shoulders, and arms were nearly identical to humans'. But below that there was nothing. No torso. No legs. No face, either, or else all these humans were faced away from us.

The humans held long sticks that they rested on the sand or held upright.

They seemed to take no notice of us. Our approach had been silent, and it was dark, and yet we were less than a quarter mile away.

"Let's take a closer look," I whispered.

We crept across the sand. Closer. Closer. Then I saw one of the squat creatures rise up. A torso and legs appeared!

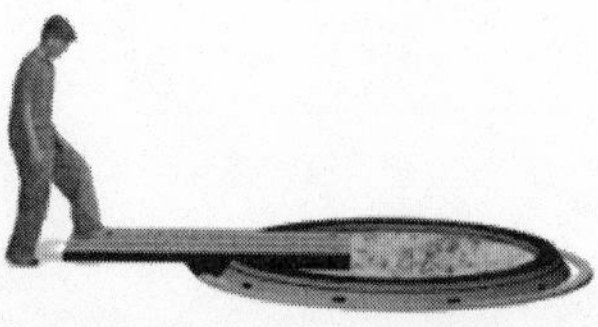

He was human. And then I realized they were all humans. They were in a series of holes, or a trench. Buried up to the chest.

"Strange behavior," I muttered.

Ka-WHUMPF!

The trench directly in front of me, less than a hundred yards distant, simply exploded. The concussion was incredible. The violence of the explosion was stunning.

Ka-WHUMPF! Ka-WHUMPF! Ka-WHUMPF!

Explosions everywhere! The humans in the trench were sent flying into the air, wrapped in flame, their bodies ripped apart.

Essam grabbed me and threw me roughly to the ground.

Ka-WHUMPF! Ka-WHUMPF! Ka-WHUMPF!

Again and again, the ground erupted. The brilliant red-and-orange explosions illuminated the night, almost blinding my vision. The ground literally struck me, leaped up with each concussion and slammed my chest.

I was frightened. I was more than frightened.

But I was watching, still, learning, trying to understand. There was a low whistle that preceded the explosions. And with my slightly damaged night vision I saw blurs of falling objects.

The explosive projectiles were coming from

overhead. Perhaps being dropped by atmospheric craft.

"They're attacking us!" Essam cried.

"No, you fool! The explosions —"

Ka-WHUMPF! Ka-WHUMPF! Ka-WHUMPF! Ka-WHUMPF!

Sand poured down like rain. Something heavy landed beside me, mere feet away. In the light of the next explosion I saw it clearly for a half second: a human torso. Arms, legs, head, all gone.

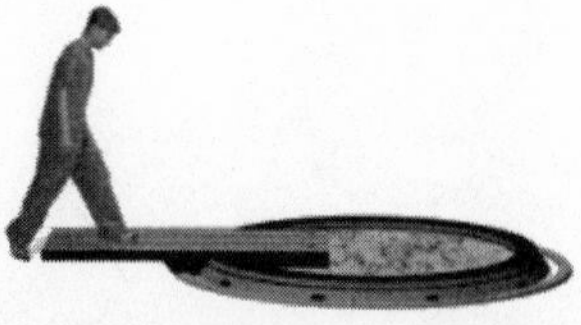

CHAPTER 7

"They aren't attacking us," I yelled. "Those humans up in the trench, *they're* the target. Watch! The explosions follow the line."

Ka-WHUMPF! Ka-WHUMPF!

Then . . . nothing. Sudden silence. Not even the sound of sand falling around us.

Finally, voices began to cry out in the night. Alien voices, but their pain and terror were clearly evident.

"Back to the ship," I ordered. I was exhilarated. It was battle, after all. Not our battle, but still with all the drama of life and death, winners and losers.

We jumped up and ran for the ship. For a moment I thought we'd become lost. The ship was nowhere to be seen.

Then, Essam pointed. Our ship had slid into a crater. A crater made by the explosions.

"Maybe they *were* after us," I said.

Essam was already running, sliding down the

sand, slamming into the ship. "Ship's computer, open the exterior hatch!" he yelled.

"Quiet! The humans will hear."

"Ship's computer, open the exterior hatch!"

"Silence! Listen!"

There was a deep, rumbling, growling sound. Growing louder. From our left. From behind the shattered trench. And now, a slightly different note, from our right.

"Something's happening," I said. "The battle isn't done. Not yet."

"Ship's computer," Essam hissed. "This is an override. Priority One. Emergency backup protocol. *Open exterior hatch*."

The hatch opened. Essam leaped inside.

I left him to worry about the ship. He was an engineer, I was not. Instead, I climbed up the side of the ship and stood there on top, with my head above the rim of the crater.

My night vision was completely restored now. I could see a line of large vehicles to my left. They were broad, squat, slow, ground-hugging machines that roared with the effort of moving their own armored weight. Between the machines were humans, hunched low, carrying sticks or poles half their own height. The poles were unmistakably weapons.

To my right, farther away, a second line of simi-

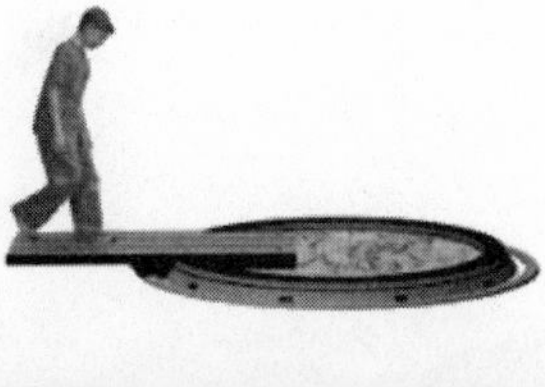

lar vehicles. Fewer in number, but slightly larger, quieter, and somewhat faster. They, like the first group, seemed to move on tracks. Very primitive.

Above these machines were low-flying ships, half a dozen or so. They beat the air with a strange rotary wing, and bristled with what could only be missiles hung on pods and arrayed along either side.

"Sub-Visser! Please come down here!" Essam called. "It's not safe out there."

"No, it definitely isn't, Essam," I said with a laugh.

"Sub-Visser, the engines are down, but I can raise our protective force field. But you'll have to come inside."

"Not yet, Essam. Not yet."

The first group of machines moved slowly, cautiously. The second group swiftly, boldly. Then it occurred to me. The first group could not see the second. They were moving blindly!

The turrets of the faster group turned. Long poles took aim. And then, from the flying machines above . . .

Woooosh!

BOOM!

The missiles fired! Right over my head they flew, trailing poorly combusted chemical fuel.

The ground machines opened fire at the same instant.

Crumpf!

BOOM!

The slower tracked machines began to explode. One. Another. Another. As each missile found its target.

BOOM! And a tracked vehicle would erupt into flame and grind to a halt. Within five minutes seventeen of the slower machines were annihilated. None of the swift, sure forces on the right were hit.

The battle swung away, north, as the leftward force began to run.

Essam emerged and climbed up beside me.

"They make war on each other?" he said. "Humans and humans?"

"Yes. So it would seem."

The battle had left me feeling conflicted. It had been wild and exhilarating! But there was a sad dimension, as well: The weapons were primitive but powerful. Given the great numbers the humans could call on, they might be formidable.

If so, if humans were too powerful to conquer, my future was death. Quick from Dracon execution, or slow from some sure-death assignment.

Essam said it out loud. "Are they Class Four, Sub-Visser?"

I shook my head. "No, Essam. I will find the way. I will find the way to conquer them. And I already know one thing."

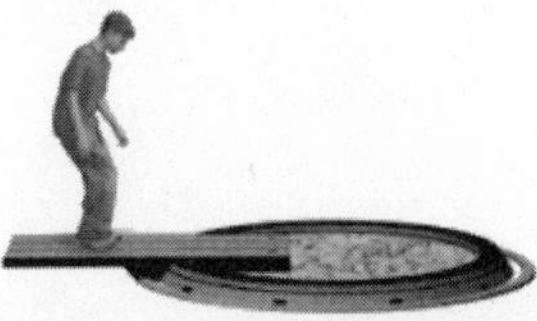

"What is that, Sub-Visser?"

I watched the swift-moving machines that even now had closed on the fleeing prey and continued its annihilation in detail, explosions like flowers in the night.

I pointed at the victors, the swift, confident pursuers. "If we want Earth, we must start with them."

CHAPTER 8

It took several hours to get our ship flying again. And now the sun was rising on a vista of bleak destruction. Sand stretched forever, a flat, tan emptiness broken up only by the scorch marks of explosions, the burned-out hulks of the tracked machines, and the occasional human corpse.

Here and there were knots of defeated humans wandering, lost.

A mile or more above the sand, swift, sleek-lined speed-of-sound atmospheric ships flew. Lower down there were the rotary-winged ships. Far to the east was a long line of the armored vehicles moving north by east.

We flew low and slow. We were safe from radar, but visual masking technology was still in its infancy and available only on a few ships. Not ours.

"What do we do, Sub-Visser?"

I didn't answer. I was scanning the ground ahead through the forward transparency and in the magnification screens.

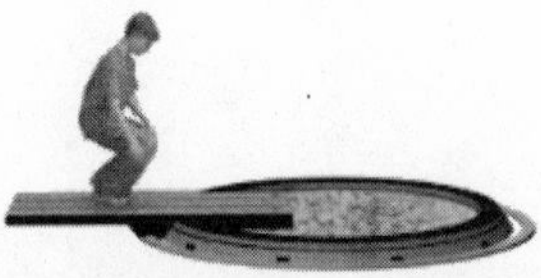

"There. Ahead and left, a human alone. Take us there, put us down close to him."

We flew toward the lone, staggering human. As we passed over he looked up and raised his arms over his head. We landed and he came toward us at a shuffling run, hands still held high.

We opened the hatch and I stepped down. The human stopped running. He stared. He yelled something in his human language and turned to run away.

Humans are not much slower than Hork-Bajir on the ground. But I was healthy, well fed, well rested. The human was none of those things. I was on him very quickly. Essam was right behind me.

The human began shouting and waving his arms, kneeling, and engaging in all manner of unfamiliar gestures. Essam and I stood over him.

"Hold him, Essam."

Essam grabbed the human's arms and pinned them behind him, locking his wrists in one big Hork-Bajir hand.

"His head, Essam. Hold his head."

"Here? You're doing it here?"

"Don't question my orders," I snapped. "Hold his head."

Essam closed his other hand over the human's head. He twisted the head till the ear, the open, inviting ear, was aimed upward, exposed.

"Your Hork-Bajir host body!" Essam hissed.

I hesitated. In my rush to enter this human I had almost forgotten. The instant I was out of my present host he would try to escape.

Escape where? That was the question. In this treeless emptiness the Hork-Bajir wouldn't get far.

I grabbed the human's head to steady it. I leaned down and pressed my own ear to his.

I began to disengage from my host's brain. I withdrew from the lesser functions first. I stretched my body out, thinning to ease through the ear canal till part of me was in contact with the human's outer ear and part of me remained in tenuous contact with the Hork-Bajir brain.

Now would come the most perilous part of the journey. I had to release my hold on the Hork-Bajir brain and would be, for a few terrible seconds, entirely vulnerable.

Every possible scenario occurred to me. That the Hork-Bajir host would grab me and kill me while I was defenseless. That the human would somehow contrive to grab me.

That Essam might kill me himself. What did he have to lose? He could claim I died in battle and then take for himself the credit for discovering a Class-Five species.

But I had no practical alternative. Besides, victory goes to the bold. I had bet my life on success.

I dropped my last contact with the Hork-Bajir. I was blind again. Half deaf. And suddenly seared by incredible heat. My slime layer was instantly dry and stiff.

I felt my way toward the human's ear canal. Slithered across the convoluted folds of the human's outer ear.

I felt the vibration of noise. No doubt the human was screaming. But I pushed on. My forward antenna array felt the darkness, the warmth, the welcome confinement ahead.

Down into that unfamiliar tunnel. I was an explorer! To the best of my knowledge no other Yeerk had ever gone where I was going: into a human.

The first, I would be the first human-Controller. My place in history was assured. My survival was not.

CHAPTER 9

I felt giddy with excitement. I would never be able to describe the sensation! The trepidation mixed with anticipation. The nervousness, almost a feeling of shyness, of being an intruder in a place where I was not allowed.

Often, in later years I wished I'd paid more attention to the details. To those first heady impressions. I wished I'd cataloged the pulsing of a human artery, the wild rush of firing neurons, the comic contortions of the human struggling to escape.

But I was too involved in the moment to form the deep, complete memories that can be replayed in infinite detail later on.

By the time I infested my first Gedd there was already a huge body of information on how best to subdue the Gedd mind. The same when it was time to move up to Hork-Bajir.

But this was all new. No one could tell me what to expect. No one could tell me what I would find

inside this new, unexplored territory, the human brain.

The ear canal was too tight, of course. There were structures in my path, small bones, a sort of timpanic membrane. I experimented with shoving them aside, rearranging them, secreting the numbing chemicals as I went.

And then, at last, there it was! Just an inch away. Nothing but a last flimsy membrane between me and the brain.

I reached. I stretched. I touched!

Flashes of auditory memory. Had to be, it wasn't real time. No, definitely memory. Memory of human voices. Several different ones. Meaningless jabber. I wasn't near the language circuitry, yet.

I spread, squeezed between skull and brain. I found deep crevices, cracks, gaps within the brain. Experimentally I reached down into one of these gaps.

There! There it was: language!

But no, no. It didn't make sense. No, it was as if I . . . yes, of course. The language functions must be dispersed in more than one area of the brain. This was a *part* of the language computer. Not all of it.

I seeped down through the crack and found myself experiencing an entirely new sense. Vague. Strange. Disturbing. No detail. It . . . it wasn't tied to specific visual or auditory memories.

It seemed to be triggered whenever the human inhaled. Yes. That was it. Through the human's breathing apparatus. But it was a useless sense. Too little specific information.

I continued my exploration. And then, suddenly, I was seeing. Seeing with eyes that were very similar to Hork-Bajir eyes. Weaker in depth perception. Stronger in color differentiation. Slow to adjust from long distance to short. But good eyes. Eyes that would serve a Class-Five species.

I turned the eyes and heard the human moan. I focused on Essam. He was still holding the human's head. Essam's Hork-Bajir face was inches from my eyes.

I turned my eyes, trying out the equipment. Left. Right. Up. Down. I spotted movement. A Hork-Bajir, running across the sand. My host body, attempting to escape.

Essam spoke. I heard too little to comprehend.

I spread further, searching for the real-time auditory input. Searching as well for motor control.

Then I discovered something strange and disturbing. A huge, deep chasm. It seemed to separate the human brain into two halves. And between the halves was only a nerve bundle not much thicker than my own true body.

Two halves? Why? Why would the human brain be divided in halves? It was irrational design. It

made no sense. Unless . . . was this a fully redundant system that would allow the creature to function in the event half its brain was destroyed?

Tentatively I reached toward the far side of the brain. I touched it. Made contact.

Fascinating!

It was incredible. This second half of the brain was an almost mirror image, but not. It could have functioned all on its own, if necessary, and yet it was in some ways radically different in its memories, its sensory interpretation, even its will. Two almost entirely functional brains in one skull, communicating across a channel of nerves. Not a fully redundant system, almost a second, *different* brain!

Why? It had to involve specialization, of some sort. And yet I found visual and auditory functions on both sides. I found memory on both sides. Found motor control on both sides.

It was then that I knew I was seeing something new. This brain worked by dialectic. Each half of the brain saw and heard and smelled and touched a slightly different world. Each tended toward specialization, but not a hard, fast split. The left half had more language, but not all the language. The right side had more spatial perception, but not all of the spatial perception.

Confusion! Disorder! Illogic!

This mind could argue with itself. This mind

could see the same event in different ways. It was insanity! A democratic brain, arguing within itself, with no sure, certain control, only a sort of uneasy compromise. A consensus of disputatious elements.

This brain contained its own traitor!

And, as I began to sift the memories I saw, again and again, the internal argument. The "Should I? Should I not?" debates. The paralysis of internal disagreement.

But I also saw decisions improved as a result of uncertainty. Hesitation and internal discord leading to decisions that were wiser, more useful, than quicker decisions would have been.

And yet that seemed a small compensation for internal treason and confusion and conflict.

No wonder they kill each other, I thought. *They very nearly kill themselves!*

It was madness. Humans, as a species, were mad.

CHAPTER 10

I took control slowly. Slowly, so that I could test each new discovery.

Once I could control motor functions I walked the human host back to the ship. Essam took us low and slow in pursuit of my Hork-Bajir host body. It was not hard to find him. He left tracks across the sand. Being Hork-Bajir it never occurred to the simple creature to try and conceal his footprints.

He kept running as we approached. Essam piloted the ship and skimmed along the sand till we could hit the Hork-Bajir with a slow-speed blow that knocked the body to the ground.

Essam tied and secured it and dragged it inside where it lay trussed in a corner, weeping and moaning in a most distracting way.

I continued my exploration of the human. I understood his senses, now: sight, sound, touch, smell, and taste. I understood his motor functions. (Wonderful hands!) I understood his language. And with this came the inevitable awareness of the human mind cowering down in a far corner of the brain, crying, blustering, threatening, begging, and praying to what this human called "Allah."

Now I was busy poring through rich, voluminous memories. Memories of family life: The creature had a wife, a sort of life partnership that was inexplicable. He had reproduced: three small humans, two male, one female. And, it seemed, humans maintained a relationship with their offspring. He had duties — a job — as a painter. He applied protective and visually appealing coverings to human structures.

But his people were poorly led and had blundered into a war they could not possibly win. And in the emergency of war he had been called to serve in the military. He was unhappy about the war, unhappy about being separated from his mate and progeny. And, at the same time, he was proud of doing his duty.

Proud that his male offspring would know that he had been a soldier.

The interest in progeny was persistent. It intruded on any number of thoughts. It formed part of the basis for the creature's sense of his place in the world.

He was confused, a split perspective that was obviously typical of humans: afraid of being killed, proud to risk being killed. The fear, at least, was familiar.

"I am finished," I said, using the human's mouth to speak to Essam.

"Finished, Sub-Visser?"

"I am finished with this human's memories. I have learned all I need for now."

"Will you keep the body or return to your Hork-Bajir host?"

"I'll return to the Hork-Bajir," I said. "This creature is useless. His people are weak. He is one of those associated with the losers in the battle we witnessed."

"Should we not begin with the weaker humans?" Essam asked. "Would they not be more vulnerable to takeover?"

I shook my new human head. "But victory in this location would be meaningless. No, Essam. When I go to the Council of Thirteen and plead for my life, I must be able to tell them that I have a plan for taking this species. And that means taking the most powerful subgroupings among them."

Essam nodded. "As you say, Sub-Visser."

"The enemies of this creature are called French, the British, the Israelis, and the Americans. Various nationalities, subgroupings of humans. They are the victors. Of those subgroupings this creature believes the most powerful to be the Americans. It is to them that we must go, Essam. So, we will go to the place called America."

CHAPTER 11

<Do we really need to go through all of this?>

The Memory Transfer Protocol faded. But my own memories of those glory days still played.

No one answered Visser Three. They were all still lost in the direct, visceral sensation of having infested a human. The memory dump allowed them to see as I had seen, feel all I had felt. I was glad they had felt it, the seductive, addictive pleasure of controlling a human. Felt the nimble fingers and the sharp senses.

<Do we really have to go through all this?> Visser Three demanded again.

Garoff snapped out of his trance and answered with more patience than was deserved. "Visser Three, you agreed that using the information from the contemporaneous memory dump was for the best."

<Yes, Council Member Garoff. But must we go through all the details of Visser One's early time on

Earth? I can point to those portions of the record that are relevant to the issue of Visser One's treason.>

Garoff laughed. It was not a friendly laugh. "Visser Three, the Council will look at the evidence Visser One chooses to submit." He leaned forward, and his black-red hood slipped back revealing his battle-scarred, ugly Hork-Bajir face. "You may appreciate the privilege when . . . *if* . . . you ever turn out to be a defendant yourself."

That was putting it plainly enough for even the fool Visser Three to grasp: He was on trial here, as much as me.

That had been my goal from the start of the trial. To become the accuser, not the accused.

I showed no emotion on my human face. No reaction. No gloating.

"Perhaps we should take a break," Garoff suggested with just a hint of hesitation. He did not glance down the line at his fellow Council members, nothing so careless. But he waited to hear whether the Emperor would object.

One of the Thirteen was Emperor. But only the Thirteen knew which one. Great leaders attract assassination threats. An Andalite assassin would have to kill all thirteen Council members to kill the Emperor himself. And the same would be true of a Yeerk assassin.

"We will adjourn for one standard hour," Garoff said.

The holographic connection was broken. The Council members disappeared. I was alone in the room with Visser Three and the ceremonial Hork-Bajir guards.

"Are you enjoying your big moment, Visser?" I smirked.

<You think you've outmaneuvered me, Edriss-Five-Six-Two? You underestimate me. You always have.>

"I understand you perfectly, Esplin-Nine-Four-Double-Six. You have the necessary brutality without the necessary subtlety. You are crude and emotional. You've made no progress with Earth. None. For all your grandiose schemes you are no further toward the goal than when you took over."

He started to answer, then stopped. He motioned to one of the Hork-Bajir and gave him some instruction.

<I know that human bodies suffer from hunger and thirst at regular intervals,> he said to me.

Moments later the Hork-Bajir reappeared with a glass of water, a head of romaine lettuce, and two raw eggs. I laughed aloud.

"So typical of you, Visser Three. You remain utterly ignorant of humans. Lettuce and raw eggs. Yes, just perfect."

I took the water and drank it down. My mouth, half-paralyzed by injury, dribbled the water down my chest.

<You may be right, Visser One,> he said. <I lack your knowledge of humans. I have never been in a human host, though I have, of course, acquired a human morph. The memory dump was . . . extraordinary. I suspect I will soon receive demands from several Council members for a shipment of human hosts. Less dangerous and powerful than Hork-Bajir hosts, but so much more enjoyable.>

I watched him cautiously. He was up to something.

He paced back and forth slowly, his hard hooves tap-tapping. <I often wonder why we . . . you and I . . . did not become allies. I even wonder at times, whether it is even now too late.>

He trained all four of his eyes on me. Waited.

"I see. You want my help?"

<Think of it as a partnership,> he said. <You and I together? With Earth and all it holds? The only known Class-Five species? Five billion, on the way to six billion potential hosts? We would command more power than all the rest of the Empire together.>

I froze. Was he suggesting what I thought he was suggesting? I waited, forcing him to commit himself.

He moved close, his hateful Andalite face, that smug, mouthless mask inches from me. <Why would we even need the rest of the Empire? Why would we need those fools on the Council? You and I together could subdue Earth and start our own, New Yeerk Empire!>

It was so surprising I almost dropped the water glass. The crudeness of the trap was insulting. Was I a fool? Was I insane?

"Visser Three, you are recording all this, of course. And of course you are recording only visual and auditory tracks. Not thought-speak. You hope to trick me into saying something treasonous so you can triumphantly play the recording back for the Council." I shook my head, pitying. "The real wonder, Visser, is that you ever rose to your present rank."

He drew back like I'd slapped him. His tail twitched, aching, desperate to swing that deadly blade and send my head rolling across the floor.

The hologram returned. The Council was assembled again. The two Taxxon members were noisily finishing a meal of something that might still be partly alive.

"Continue Memory Transfer Protocol," Garoff

ordered and once more I was plunged back into my own past. Back to the magical, wondrous days when I was taking my first humans.

Back to the days when all the galaxy was going to be mine.

CHAPTER 12

Stored Memory Transfer Protocol

We disposed of my first host. I returned to my Hork-Bajir host body and we flew back into orbit.

Finding a particular place called America was not easy. My short-lived host was not an educated human and had had only a vague notion. Earth's landmasses have various distinguishing features: mountain ranges, rivers, valleys, lakes, coastlines, and so on, but nothing that makes clear that a particular collection of rivers and mountains is one nation and not another.

I returned to the tedious job of searching the raging torrent of electronic data. I detailed the computer to search for references to "America." There were billions.

But slowly, as our food and water supply dwindled dangerously, I began to piece together a few facts. America was a geographic entity defined on the west, east, and southeast by ocean. The northern border seemed arbitrary. The southwestern border was defined primarily by an otherwise insignificant river.

Humans speak many languages. Americans primarily spoke a language called "English."

So I used the computer to filter out all non-English language data. Still the data stream was overwhelming. I began to arbitrarily dismiss entire genres of data: voice only, telemetry, the rhythmic pulsations that humans call music.

I focused on the combined voice-music-visual signals known as television.

Now I had a basis for proceeding. Or so I thought. But television data was confusing. Some seemed to be simple recordings of events. Others, however, were artificially colored, or artificially drained of color. Some portrayed creatures that were unlikely to exist in nature.

I wished I'd kept the human host.

"Sub-Visser, the water situation has become critical," Essam said. "I must leave this host body within hours, unless we obtain water."

"Soon, Essam. Hold on a bit longer."

I plunged back into the television data, with a particular emphasis on military technology. So confusing. At times it seemed that humans were armed with simple bows that fired sharpened sticks by means of tension produced by a stretched string.

Other times they seemed to possess mostly small handheld weapons that made loud sounds and apparently fired small, high-velocity projectiles. On occasion they possessed no weapons at all but relied on swift physical blows.

And then, to my horror, I began to see evidence that human military potential was far greater than anything I'd expected: In some of the television data they possessed nuclear fusion explosives. And in other data they were shown using highly effective, adjustable-intensity beam weapons they called "phasers."

"Faster-than-light spacecraft? Faster-than-light through real space? Impossible!" Essam said, looking over my shoulder. "And armed with beam weapons?"

"How do they manage to get visual records of ships moving at faster-than-light speeds? See, there! The ship is announced to be moving at Warp-Factor Six, which we know from context is a multiple of light speed. And yet there we see the ship from the outside, as though the recording device, too, is moving at these impossible speeds."

"Not possible," Essam said, his voice rasping, his tongue dry. I had drunk the last of the water several hours earlier.

"No. Faster-than-light travel is an impossibility.

Not even the Andalites can do it! That is why we tunnel into Zero-space."

I was puzzled. Confused. Was it possible . . . were the humans creating these images to frighten away potential enemies? Was that it? Was this all a complex bluff designed to intimidate potential conquerors?

Then, it hit me in a flash of insight. "It's all a lie, Essam. It's not real. These are created events! Simulations! The humans, they . . . they invent these events."

"But what for, Sub-Visser?"

"To intimidate us, Essam. Or . . . or perhaps for some other reason. None of what we see in this data can be taken at face value. There are elements of artifice and deception in all of it!"

"How can we differentiate? How do we know what's real and what's not?"

"We can't," I admitted, once more frustrated. "Perhaps a human can, but it will take us years to sift data in order to determine which weapons systems and capabilities are real and which are simulated. Even the simple matter of human social structure is inexplicable. They have forms of interaction that defy analysis!"

"Yes, they are unusual, certainly. I . . . nothing."

"What, Essam? What have you learned?"

He shook his head. "The data seems to show humans simultaneously bound in tight, emotion-based relationships, and yet quite likely to murder each other. On occasion they kill each other at an artificially slow speed."

"Once again, we cannot learn what we need from orbit. There is too little time. We must plunge boldly into the shallow end of the pool, Essam. Boldness is called for."

"The last attempt was inadequate."

"I did not then understand the geography of Earth," I said, annoyed at his implied criticism. "I have learned. It is still confusing, but I know this: Even within the limited geographic and political entity called 'America' there are further subdivisions. Cities. Some are obviously irrelevant. Only four are mentioned frequently in the data: New York, Washington DeeCee, Ellay, and Hollywood. Of these I conclude from the prevalence of mentions in the data that Hollywood is the most important."

I stood up and pushed back from the computer console. "We'll get your water, Essam. The time has come for a second visit to *my* planet."

CHAPTER 13

I had absorbed much of the English language. I could recognize and interpret the written form of the language. And as I swooped down on the glittering human city below, I saw the letters, high on a hilltop: Hollywood.

It was almost as if the humans had expected to be visited from space and had placed the letters there to guide us.

We landed in a deep valley in the hills above the city. Our Hork-Bajir bodies were admirably suited for clambering up the steep canyon sides, so much like the Hork-Bajir home world.

We emerged near a building placed on stilts, jutting out precariously over the canyon. It was brightly illuminated. And a large, ovoid pool of water was brightly lit as well.

We stood in the shadows beyond the pool. It was the size of the sort of pool one might find aboard one of the newer Pool ships. It could have

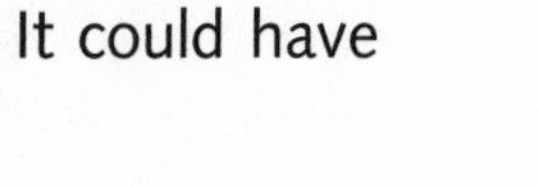

housed ten thousand Yeerks, if necessary. Of course it was mere water, and horribly transparent at that.

"There is your water, Essam."

We brushed aside a row of sticks that may have been intended as some sort of primitive defensive barrier. Essam ran to the water, knelt down, and plunged his face into it.

Suddenly, from the far end of the pool, a human emerged! A human female wearing a very minimal garment in two pieces.

"Oh, wow!" she cried.

I raised my Dracon beam. Essam jerked up from the water. I thought he was responding to the presence of this unexpected human. But he began to scream and clutch at his face.

"Aaaarrrgghh!"

"Oh, man, are you guys, like, from the studio?"

"Essam! What is the difficulty?"

He staggered, big Hork-Bajir talons pressed against his face. "It burns! It burns!"

"The pool guy was here, today," the woman said. "The chlorine's always kind of high right after. Um, should I get Lonnie? I mean, Mr. Lowenstein? He's making drinks."

"It burns! It burns!" Essam cried.

"Silence, Essam!" I snapped. To the woman, I said, "You are a female."

She made a human mouth gesture. And she twisted her body slightly, pressing some portions forward aggressively. "I hope I'm a woman," she said.

A second human emerged from the building. A male. Shorter than the female. Also thicker. And partially covered with thin, curly fur. He carried two small, transparent, open containers that appeared to hold liquid.

"Hey! What are you doing here? How'd you get in here?"

"The studio sent them," the female supplied.

The male nodded and looked closely at us. "That's good work, but the look is all wrong. This is way too *Alien* for what I need. I was looking for something more *E.T.* Cute, cuddly. Not blades and chicken feet."

Essam seemed to be surviving his exposure to the chlorine. "Essam, we'll take these two."

He wiped his eyes with the back of his fingers. "Which one do you prefer for yourself, Sub-Visser?"

I considered. The male was larger and more powerful. But he was also slower in his movements, less agile. Older, I concluded. Perhaps near death. The female seemed healthier.

"I will take the female," I said.

Essam moved swiftly. He grabbed the female and held her as he had held the lost soldier in the desert.

"Hey! Hey! What the . . . hey! You're not from the studio!" the male shouted. "I'm calling the cops. Then, I'm calling my lawyer!"

He turned and ran back into the building.

I went to the female and swiftly, easily now that I had experience, took control of her. A few minutes later Essam took the man.

Thus I became female. And Essam became male. And when the "cops" arrived they found nothing suspicious.

Our two Hork-Bajir hosts had disappeared. Their atoms scattered in the atmosphere of Earth by our Dracon beams.

We had, in the human expression, burned our bridges.

CHAPTER 14

We stood, awkward, in the middle of a large, open room adorned with objects made of chrome, glass, and stretched, denuded animal pelts bleached white. On the walls were framed woven fibers covered with colors applied for the purpose of visual pleasure.

My host's name was Jenny-Lynne Cadwalader. Everyone called her Jenny Lines. She was twenty-three years of age. I did a quick search of her memories and found little of interest there.

Her reaction to the infestation was to whine and complain. She did not scream or rage. She did not threaten. She merely subsided into a corner and occasionally remarked that I was a "total jerk."

Jenny had no occupation, a concept that shocked my Yeerk sensibilities. She considered herself an actress — one of the humans who pretend to be people they are not in dishonest TV or movie representations. But though she called herself an actress, she had never acted.

From early on in my possession of the host I became aware of the fact that there was really only one thing that interested her. She was very deeply interested in a particular mood-altering chemical.

As I wrapped myself around her brain and sank deep around her corpus callosum — the bridge between brain halves — Jenny demanded to know whether I would supply her needs for this drug.

I ignored her, of course. There is very little point in engaging in internal conversation with a host. One might as well be talking to one's self, except in rare cases. And in the case of Jenny Lines I might have had more enjoyable conversations with a ship's computer.

"This host is quite ignorant, I believe," I remarked to Essam once the police were gone.

<Hey! Who are you calling ignorant?>

"Yes, my host agrees that she is quite ignorant," Essam said. "However, my host finds her desirable."

"Desirable? How so?"

"She is considered physically attractive. It is a subjective evaluation based on visual memory and tied to the human's procreative instincts."

I considered. Searching the memory I discovered the location of a device that allows a human to view his physical self in reflection. A mirror behind a shelf that held numerous small glass containers designed to hold liquids.

I walked to the mirror. I looked at the physical body. It did not excite any particular sense of aesthetic pleasure in me. And yet Jenny Lines was confident that she was attractive.

<I'm hotter than half these so-called actresses. I mean, have you really looked at Sarah Jessica Parker?>

"Physical attraction. Yes, that explains a large percentage of this host's memories," I said.

"Your host has a physical addiction to a particular chemical compound," Essam said. "Mine does not. He is concerned for her."

"Concerned? Why?"

Essam shrugged large, hairy shoulders. "It is an emotion, not susceptible to logical explanation."

"Ah."

"This is my first human," Essam said cautiously. "But they appear, based on the memories I have accessed, to be widely differentiated. Male and female, young and old, wide differences in intelligence, wide differences in experience, in occupation. For example, my host's memory catalogs hundreds of possible human occupations: producer, director, actor, assistant director, gaffer, best boy, pool boy, driver, wardrobe assistant, caterer, studio head, banker, car detailer, therapist, East Coast money guy . . . many, many occupations."

"My own host's memories are deficient in infor-

mation," I confessed. "There are memories of youth spent in a place known as Cow Town or Podunk or Arkansas, with the three terms roughly synonymous, and yet also referencing multiple fictional locations. I sense a fundamental lack of organization here in this brain."

I was disappointed. My second human host and again I had chosen poorly. I wondered if anything could be accomplished with this uneducated, uninformed creature. I needed a guide to humans. This female was a guide to nothing. Except . . . except when I looked past the cataloged memories of events and interactions, the pointless conversations and drug usage and dull activities, and looked into more obscured memories.

There, deep in this shallow mind, in memories that were confused and disorganized and often deprived of obvious meaning, I found something vital.

"They have many weaknesses," I told Essam.

"Yes," he agreed. "This host is aware of many human weaknesses and exploits them for his own purposes. 'People wanna laugh,' for example. They want to escape from the reality of their lives and imagine themselves in unlikely situations. They are 'suckers' for a lot of teeth and long legs. My host has become very successful among humans by creating entertainments devised to cause laughter among humans."

I heard Essam's words, but I paid him little attention. I was excited by my own discoveries. Rooting through the memories of this abject failure of a human I began to see the glimmer of a plan to take Earth.

"I don't think that making humans laugh is our true path to the conquest of Earth," I said. "There are other needs. They are afraid, these humans. They are lonely. They are weak. So weak! This host is not much more intelligent than a Hork-Bajir!"

Essam shook the large head of his host body, already beginning to adopt human characteristics, as a good Yeerk should do when in a host. "I see things besides weakness, here," he said. "This human has suffered what the humans consider to be the most horrific torture and deprivation in their history. An experience in his youth that even a Taxxon would find cruel."

He tried out his host body's walk as he spoke. Step, step. Then he added a swinging arm motion.

"He is not from this country, originally," Essam said. "Nevertheless, he has risen to a position of power and influence among humans. I believe he has weaknesses, but is not weak, Sub-Visser."

I laughed with Jenny's mouth. "No, Essam, you are wrong. They are not a strong species with a few weaknesses. They are weak, with but a few strengths. Let me tell you, Essam: We will not have

to conquer humans. They will conquer themselves. They will come to us willingly and make themselves our slaves."

I laughed again, savoring the whimpering, nitwit cries of my host's addled mind. Jenny Lines was a revelation. She had showed me the truth and the way.

End of Stored Memory Transfer
Protocol Download 7123450.989.

CHAPTER 15

"An underestimation of the humans, would you not agree, Visser One?" Garoff asked. "These many years later, Earth is still not ours."

I was still lost in the haze of happy memory. Still back in those early, heady moments when I saw a future so bright it almost blinded me.

"No, it is not ours," I admitted in a whisper. Then I snapped myself out of my trance. "Earth is not ours because of the incompetence and treason of Visser Three. I left Earth in a position to be taken!"

<You left Earth before the Andalites landed a force of trained guerillas and saboteurs armed with morphing technology!> Visser Three cried.

There it was. Was it time to reveal what I knew of the so-called Andalite bandits? Would it ever be time?

<Go ahead, tell him,> Eva jeered inside my head. <Let Visser Three take all the glory for wiping out the "Andalite bandits.">

<Soon I will make you suffer for this, Eva.>

If Earth was mine again, I would make short work of the so-called Andalites. But if I was to lose this trial, if I was to be exiled or executed and Visser Three left to control Earth . . . well, if that was to be the case, I'd rather die far from the nearest Kandrona than give Visser Three the information he needed to secure Earth.

"It would seem that Essam was more correct than you in his assessment of humans," Garoff prodded. "While many humans have come willingly to us, many more do not. And we see reports of large numbers of host problems with humans. We have reports of Yeerks driven to lose control under the constant internal pressure of a resistant human host."

I bristled at the criticism. "At that early point we did not understand humans. I had encountered only two humans through infestation: a defeated soldier, and a weakling in thrall to a chemical."

<Nonsense,> Visser Three jumped in. <You had, by your own admission, realized that humans are widely differentiated as a species. You had every reason to suspect that humans could be resistant to your notion of conquest by infiltration. You deliberately overlooked that fact. You *chose* to underestimate the humans. You chose to ignore the more obvious fact that humans can be bludgeoned and

cowed into submission, and those who resist can simply be exterminated.>

"Had I infested the Lowenstein host I would have seen sooner what I soon saw anyway," I said, holding my temper with difficulty. "But I was still more right than wrong. Humans are riddled with exploitable weaknesses. Humans, at least some humans, will believe anything: They will surrender their free will to addictive chemical compounds, to strong-willed leaders, to their own greed for power. . . . It was from this insight that I realized the concept of The Sharing. How many thousands of humans have in fact come to us voluntarily? Submitted to us for empty promises of happiness or wealth or status?"

<How many thousands?> Visser Three mocked. <Not enough! *You* set the policy of conquest by infiltration. The time has come for all-out attack! A war of conquest! Destroy their military power, seize their leaders, herd them into the vast pools we will build, infest them in their hundreds of thousands, in their millions, in their billions!>

So that was it. That was Visser Three's goal: all-out war. No! I couldn't allow that! It would result in the deaths of millions, which was irrelevant to me, but it might also result in the deaths of two. Two humans I would not allow to be killed!

I stood up and shook my mangled fist at Visser

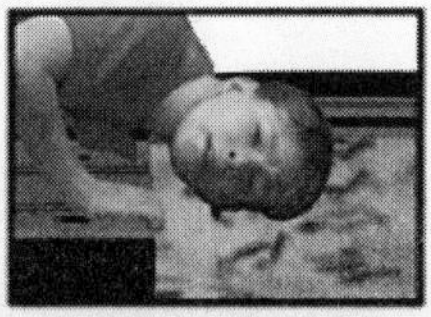

Three. "This fool would strip away the secrecy that has allowed us to make progress on Earth. We cannot hope to win an easy victory over a population of billions!"

<There! There is her treason, clearly stated! She would have us hide and creep and crawl forever, when we should be attacking! She is inventing excuses to delay our takeover, stalling for time till the Andalites, her masters, can come to the rescue of Earth!>

"I *gave* us Earth! I *found* it! There would have been no Earth but for me! I created The Sharing and drew tens of thousands of human hosts into our reach. All without ever alarming the human authorities. I found the way, the path, to eventually seizing five billion hosts, all with a mere handful of Yeerks! I handed this all to Visser Three, and what has he done with it? That, Council members, that is the question we —"

I saw Visser Three's tail whip around. I ducked, cried out in rage, slipped to the floor, stifling the screams of agony as some of my imperfectly healed bones were rebroken.

But it was not me he was attacking.

Two of the Hork-Bajir guards had suddenly gone mad! One yanked open the door to the room. The other drew his Dracon weapon and fired at me.

Tseeeeeeew!

The shot missed only because I had jerked away from Visser Three.

The remaining Hork-Bajir were staring blankly like statues.

"Get them, you fools!" I screamed.

Then, through the door, a flash of orange and black. Big, bigger than a human, and so fast!

The tiger landed, barely touched the floor with its soft pads and leaped straight for Visser Three. It flew! And it let loose a roar that reached past me, past my control of my human host, down deep into the human subconscious with a jolt of sheer terror.

"HRRROOOOAAAARRRR!"

A second roar, rougher, more of a hoarse cough joined the first and a bear so huge it dwarfed the Hork-Bajir barreled awkwardly, almost unwillingly, into the room.

"What is happening?" Garoff demanded from his position of safety many light-years distant.

<The Andalite bandits!> Visser Three cried.

Instantly I realized: an opportunity! The so-called Andalite bandits had attacked! How better to show Visser Three's impotence, his weakness!

It would destroy Visser Three's shredded credibility. And I would be the victor!

If I lived.

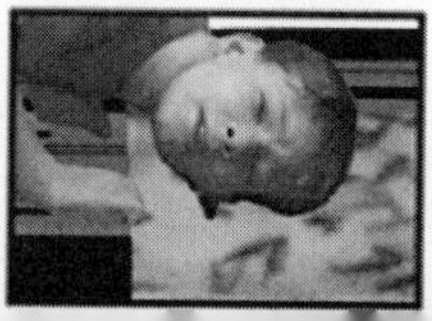

CHAPTER 16

The grizzly bear reared up and slammed two Hork-Bajir against a wall. Slammed them so hard that the wind was knocked out of them and blood trickled from their mouths.

The two bandits in Hork-Bajir morph were slashing viciously, left, right.

I scrambled, half-crawling across the floor, looking for a Dracon weapon. Visser Three whipped his Andalite tail and swiped off the right arm of one of the false Hork-Bajir.

Four of them: two Hork-Bajir, the tiger, the bear.

Four.

No, that was wrong. There were at least six, not four. Where were the other two? Most of all, in virtually every record we had of the bandits, one of them had usually appeared as an Andalite.

There were all sorts of theories to explain this: This one Andalite did not possess the morphing power, or else the Andalites felt they needed to keep one of their people in true form as a way to "show the flag."

I knew, or at least guessed the truth: The always-visible Andalite was a deception to keep us from realizing that at least some of the six were humans.

Where was the Andalite as Andalite?

Where were the other two?

No time for speculation. I needed a weapon. Had to show I was in the fight. Had to demonstrate my eagerness to kill. Any hesitation would condemn me in the eyes of the Council.

I reached a fallen Hork-Bajir and yanked the unfired Dracon beam from his stiffening fingers, aimed at the tiger, and fired. Missed! My twisted bones had betrayed me.

The Council of Thirteen were shouting, avid spectators at a battle to the death.

"Behind you!"

"Strike! Strike!"

I braced for the tiger to turn on me. But he seemed unaware that I had fired. He was, instead, preparing to attack Visser Three.

I prepared to fire again. It would be perfect! I would save the fool's life for him.

The bear was cough-roaring and now dropped to all fours. It hesitated, blinked, looked around as if lost.

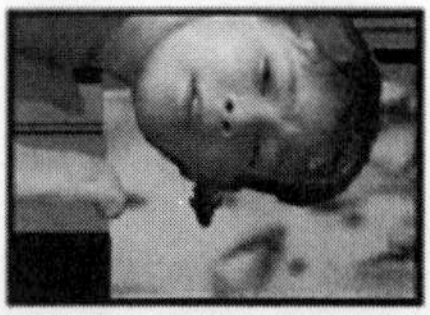

And then, to my amazement, the tiger whipped around, lightning quick, and slashed bloody tracks across the face of the bear.

Visser Three's tail whipped.

Fwapp!

Thud! The tiger's head, severed, fell to the floor.

<No! No!> Eva screamed.

Two Hork-Bajir targeted the confused, hesitant bear and fired!

Tseeeeew! Tseeeeew!

The bear sizzled, atoms burning, burst into flame for a brief, gratifying moment, bellowed a terrified roar, and disintegrated.

I saw it all now in a moment of sickening realization.

Fake! All of it false.

I had underestimated Visser Three. I could see through the falseness, now. But the fascinated Council members who had watched the bloody battle from safety knew nothing of Earth or Earth animals.

One of the "enemy" Hork-Bajir raced at Visser Three. The Visser calmly sidestepped, dropped his tail blade, and the Hork-Bajir fell hard, unable to walk further on only one leg.

The Hork-Bajir looked up stupidly at Visser Three, confused, alarmed, eyes pleading in horror at the realization that he had been betrayed.

The Visser killed him.

I almost laughed. Idiot! I wanted to yell. Did you really think Visser Three could afford to let you live?

The remaining Hork-Bajir "traitor" saw what had happened, turned to run, and was caught halfway through the door.

What could I do? Try and tell the Council that these were not the Andalite bandits? Try and tell them that Visser Three had merely had a starved tiger and bear thrust into the room? A real tiger, a real bear, and neither in any way an Andalite bandit in morph?

How would I prove that, any more than I could prove that the supposed Hork-Bajir "morphs" were simply Hork-Bajir-Controllers ordered by Visser Three to fake an attack?

I met Visser Three's gaze. I nodded grimly. *Yes, Visser,* I thought, *this game goes to you.*

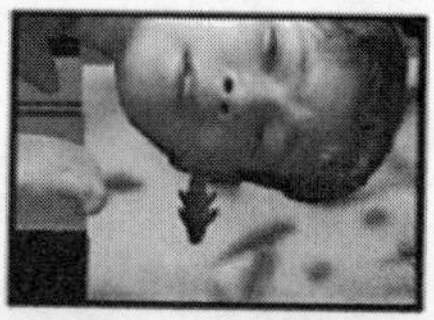

CHAPTER 17

It was devastating. My charge that Visser Three was incompetent rested on his inability to cope with the bandits.

I'd lost that, now. Now Visser Three could claim a bright future for Earth. With the resistance gone, he could do as he pleased. The Council would be drawn to the easy answer.

Gedd attendants were already dragging the corpses from the room and mopping up the blood.

I had one hope now. Only one: the real bandits. If they were to attack now the Council would realize that Visser Three had staged a charade.

It was almost a pity that I wasn't a traitor. If I were I'd have been able to call upon them for help. As it was, I knew the location of one of the guerillas. But there was no opportunity for me to reach the boy Marco. And less than no chance that he would do anything to help me.

By the most terrible coincidence, he had become an enemy. He'd been present at the destruction of the shark project. And he'd been there on a mountaintop where Visser Three and I fought to destroy a colony of free Hork-Bajir and each other.

<You underestimated my son,> my host said proudly.

<I'll kill him yet, human.>

<No,> my host said. <I believe your killing days are over.>

I could make no answer. Garoff was speaking.

"Congratulations, Visser Three. It would seem you have gone a long way toward eliminating the bandit threat there on Earth."

<It was my hope that they would attack,> Visser Three said with insincere modesty. <I deliberately planted the seeds of this moment, knowing they'd be unable to resist such a prime target. I am pleased you were able to witness the elimination of the only resistance on Earth.>

"Yes, yes," Garoff said. "And the timing was, of course, fortunate."

Visser Three said nothing in response.

I felt a surge of renewed hope. Garoff, at least, was not blind. He didn't trust this coincidence.

Good. Good. If only I could reach Marco and entice him to launch an attack. Should the real bandits show up, Visser Three's charade — and life — would be over.

"Let us return to the matter before us," Garoff

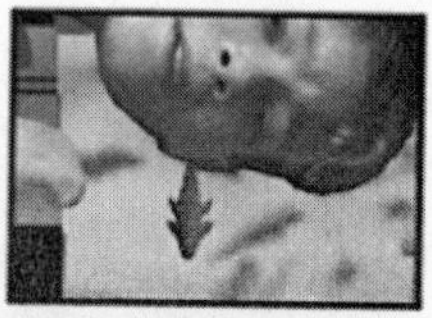

said. "Visser One, you will continue your presentation. I understand that we have a gap between Memory Transfer Protocols?"

"Yes, I —"

<A most suspicious gap,> Visser Three interrupted. <More than a year during which the defendant made no memory dumps, and never once contacted the Yeerk High Command. Fourteen Earth months during which she contacted the Andalites and hatched her conspiracy!>

"Do you have any evidence of this, Visser Three?" Garoff asked calmly.

<Yes. I have the testimony of someone who was close to Visser One during that critical time.>

"A witness? Who?"

<Essam-Two-Nine-Three.>

I tried not to show any reaction. "Surely the Visser knows that Essam is dead."

Visser Three looked away from the hologram. He smiled the unsettling Andalite smile that is done with eyes alone. <No, Visser One. Essam-Two-Nine-Three is not dead. At least not entirely. Guards! Bring in the witness.>

The door opened. In walked a human male. He was in his middle years. His dark hair was long and matted. His full steel-gray beard was greasy and stringy. His eyes had a wild look. His clothing announced him as a street person.

None of which meant a thing to the Council members. They had no experience of humans. They did not understand that this sort of human could be found in the alleyway of any large city, drinking alcohol and ranting wildly about imagined conspiracies.

I sneered dismissively. "Visser Three is perhaps jesting. This is what the humans call a 'street crazy.' A wild man, a lunatic, an alcohol addict. If this is Essam, let Essam withdraw from the host body and show himself."

<No, you are correct, of course, Visser One. The Yeerk Essam is dead. I was having a little joke. But a part of him lives on. Yes, this human is quite mad. But the question is this: *Why* is he insane? From where came his madness?>

Garoff hesitated, sensing a trick. "I hope you are not wasting the time of the Council, Visser Three. Proceed. But be warned."

The madman stared hard at Visser Three, rocked back on his heels, stared again, peering as if Visser Three were far off or concealed in a fog. Then the human looked pleadingly at me.

"It's an Andalite. You see him, don't you?"

I refused to answer.

"You all see him, don't you?" Then he took notice of the Hork-Bajir guards standing impassively against the back of the room. The wounded guards had been replaced by fresh troops.

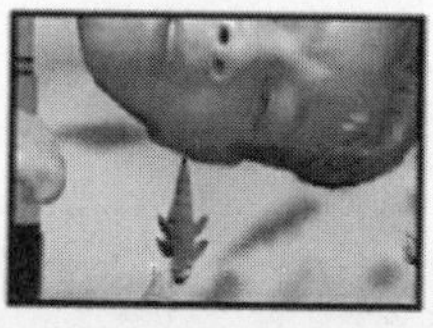

"Hork-Bajir!" the human said. He pointed here, there, his eyes wide and now brimming with tears. "Real! They're real. They are. See? See?"

<Human, what is your name?> Visser Three demanded.

"Look! They're real, all real. Lady, look!"

<I asked your name. Answer me and I will give you a fresh bottle.>

The man licked his lips. His eyes darted from me to Visser Three, to the holograms of the Council, to the Hork-Bajir guards.

"A bottle. Okay. Okay. My friends call me Spacey. Folks all do."

<Good. Spacey. Now I'm going to ask you some questions, Spacey. You will answer me. If you answer all my questions I will give you a bottle. If you attempt to lie I will kill you. Is that clear?>

Spacey nodded, more confused than afraid. His eyes kept drifting over to me, silently begging me to see what he saw, to acknowledge the presence of what he considered aliens.

<Does the name Essam mean anything to you?>

"Yes. Essam-Two-Nine-Three of the Sulp Niar pool."

Several of the Council members muttered. My brain was running at hyper speed. What was going on? What was Visser Three's game? Who was this filthy human?

<And who . . . *what* was Essam-Two-Nine-Three?>

Spacey looked doubtful. No doubt waiting for the laughter and derision he'd heard often in his years of madness. "He's a Yeerk. They come from . . . well, you all know where they come from."

<And is it true that Essam made you his host? That he took control of your brain?>

Spacey nodded. "In my ear, into my brain. Couldn't do anything on my own. Nothing. Not move my hands. Not look where I wanted to look."

<Nevertheless, you and Essam became . . . what is the word? You became friends?>

He nodded. "Much as a human can be with a Yeerk. We talked. Me and him. We were together for a long while."

Visser Three nodded. <In fact, you were his host for a year, were you not?>

I felt a strange trickle of fear. But no . . . no . . .

<And while you were his host did you know another Yeerk who had the name of Edriss-Five-Six-Two and the rank of Sub-Visser Four-hundred-nine?>

Spacey's face was split by a smile that revealed a row of broken and rotting teeth. "You mean Allison. Allison Kim."

My heart stopped beating. The blood froze in my human veins. Suddenly I saw through the mat-

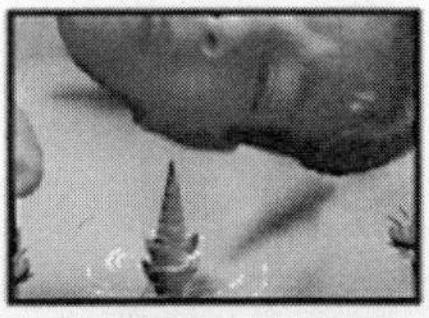

ted hair, the filthy beard, the lunatic eyes. I saw through the years.

"Oh yes, I remember her," the human said. "See, she was Essam's wife. He was in love with her."

Visser Three lowered his thought-speak voice to an insinuating whisper. <And she, this Allison Kim, this Edriss-Five-Six-Two, this Sub-Visser Four-hundred-nine, she was in love with him as well?>

"Yes, yes, Essam was sure of that. Mostly, anyway. See, if he hadn't been sure he'd never have gone ahead with it."

<With what?>

"The babies. Their kids. See, they had kids. Twins. A little girl and a little boy."

CHAPTER 18

Silence.

Dead silence.

I had to deny it. Claim that it was all a lie. Claim that Visser Three had merely given this creature a script filled with fabrications.

But was there proof? That was the question. Was there proof? The penalty for lying to the Council was horrifying.

Was Visser Three bluffing? Did he have more?

"Is this true?" Garoff asked quietly.

Eva, my host, erupted violently, horrified by this news. <You created human children to be enslaved by Yeerks? If there's a hell you'll be there soon!>

I kept my face as blank as I could manage under the assault of my host's emotions. Not to mention my own.

"Yes, Council Member Garoff. It is true that I took a human female named Allison Kim as a host. Essam took a host named Hildy Gervais."

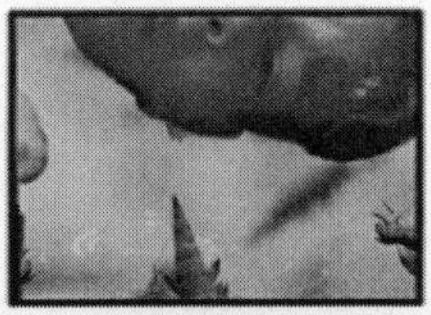

<You'll die, Edriss. I'll watch you die and laugh and thank God for the pain!>

"That's *my* name," Spacey said. "Hildy Gervais."

"And did you really cause your host bodies to reproduce?" Garoff demanded incredulously.

"Yes."

Garoff's face was hidden by the Council member's hood. But I could read the stiffening of his limbs as evidence of his reaction. The entire Council seemed to draw back.

<What we always missed was the motive,> Visser Three hissed. <It never made sense that the great Visser One, the Yeerk who had shown us Earth, who had taken us to the first Class-Five species ever discovered, would betray her own people and become a tool of the Andalites.>

"Never!" I cried. "I never was anything but an enemy to the Andalite race!"

<The truth will not set you free, Yeerk. They will never believe you. Never!>

<Shut up! Shut up!>

"You will need to explain this," Garoff said.

"I will be happy to explain." I tried to project confidence. But I was shattered. I was now close enough to Visser Three's torture chamber to be able to hear my own screams. And all the while, Eva taunted and laughed, shaking my concentration.

How to explain? How to explain that for more than a year I set aside my loyalty to my own people? How to explain that yes, for a year, I was a traitor?

"I will resume my story," I said shakily.

<This ought to be good.>

"Essam and I had made hosts of Lowenstein and Jenny Lines. They were useful. Useful for learning more about the humans. Lowenstein was a television producer. He created entertainments. Jenny Lines had been a casual acquaintance. Now that both were hosts, we naturally kept them in close contact. Jenny Lines showed me the lower elements of human society. The drug dealers, the petty criminals, the weak and feckless creatures like herself. But I tired of that. What I needed was to understand humans. To be able to assess their weaknesses on a larger scale. I needed to know for certain: Were humans Class Five or Class Four? Could we take them?"

All that sounded sensible. Logical. Reasonable.

I tried to calm my hammering human heart. Tried not to focus on the fact that Visser Three had caught me entirely by surprise.

And what else might he know? How many other witnesses might he call against me?

Only one way out, now. Marco. My host body's son. Marco, the gentle, sweet child who had obvi-

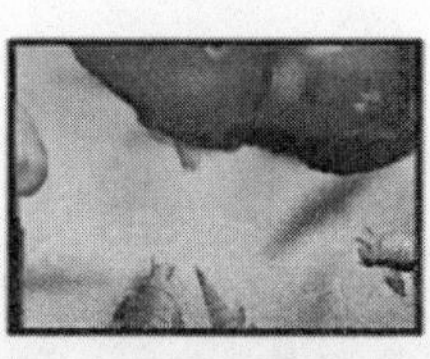

ously become something more. But I would never be allowed to communicate with him. No chance. No chance at all, unless, somehow, they were to attack on their own.

<Sad, isn't it? You need my son to save you.>

I didn't have the energy to shut her up. To argue. To threaten. I was scared. I was cornered. I was one wrong word away from a long, slow, agonizing death.

But I wasn't dead, yet. Not yet. I smiled at Visser Three. No reason. Just to make him wonder. And then, I let my memory swim back to that long-ago past.

"I happened to encounter Allison Kim at a studio party. She was the technical advisor on a television series Lowenstein produced. A series involving, appropriately enough, a human future that involved Earth being invaded by aliens.

"Allison Kim was different than Jenny Lines. She was not a drug addict. She was not stupid. She was a scientist. Oh, I know, the idea of human science is almost laughable, but she had the disciplined habits of mind, and the imagination to . . ." I hesitated. Reformulated what I was about to say. "She was more similar to the human Lowenstein than to Jenny Lines or the hapless soldier.

"I took her in the swimming pool. It was a perfect opportunity. Jenny Lines was physically strong when under my control. But she was under the influence of a number of chemicals and —"

Garoff interrupted. "You continued your human host's use of addictive chemicals?"

"Of course. It made her the perfect host in many ways. No annoying petty resistance. At one time I considered that addicts would make a perfect starting point for our invasion: They are inherently weak and susceptible. Easily taken. Unfortunately, they were also humans devoid of accomplishment or influence. They could not give us access to the levers of power."

"Continue," Garoff said.

"The water environment of the swimming pool was perfect. In this particular part of Earth, swimming pools are very common, and they are a central feature of outdoor parties."

I closed my eyes, savoring the moment. Remembering a time when I was not an accused prisoner.

Allison Kim happened to be in the swimming pool, along with one or two other humans. But Allison was in the deep end. The other two were sitting on the shallow steps.

I dived into the pool. I had made my decision

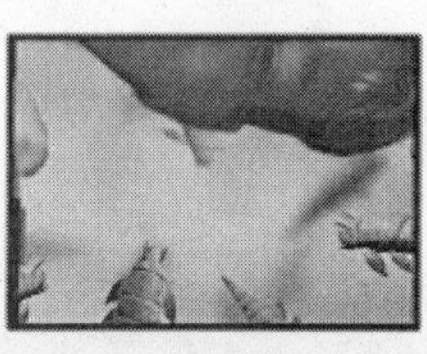

almost impetuously. I didn't know if I'd have such an opportunity later. Strike now, I told myself.

It was night. Stars peeking through above, the lights of Los Angeles a glittering carpet down below us. The pool was lit, but water distorts human vision. Things that are solid appear to wiggle and squirm.

I dived in, surfaced just behind Allison Kim. I grabbed her around the waist and pulled her down under the water.

Anyone who'd seen us, and there were dozens and dozens of humans around the pool, would have thought I was engaging in a game of some sort.

Allison thought so. Then she realized I wasn't letting her surface. I punched her hard in the stomach, forcing the air out of her lungs. I punched her in the side of the head, stunning her.

I held her head close and kicked my way down to the bottom of the pool. She struggled, but Jenny Lines was younger and stronger and an expert swimmer.

I pressed our ears together and reached out to her. It was Lowenstein's pool, so we had long since dispensed with the chlorine that would have burned my slime coat.

I reached to her across a gap of sun-warmed water. Entered her ear. Pushed with expert ease down her ear canal. Around the bones and through the membranes till I touched her mind.

All I needed was contact with her motor functions. I found them quickly enough. Tapped into her arm and leg controls. Froze her, paralyzed her.

Then, I began to disengage from Jenny Lines. I withdrew from that empty brain, keeping just one control contact till the very end. Stretched now between the two humans, half-touching Allison, half-touching Jenny, I gave a last instruction to Jenny Lines.

I made Jenny breathe.

Then I broke contact forever. Allison Kim, the new me, waited till it was too late, then made a show of hauling Jenny Lines to the surface.

I performed the primitive human methodology for resuscitating a person who has attempted to breathe water. It failed as, of course, it must.

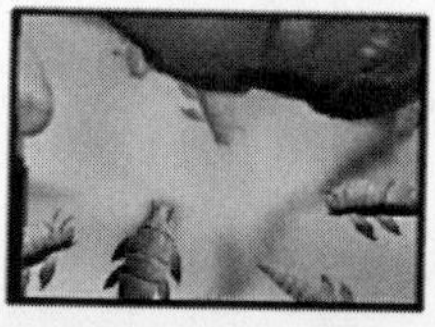

CHAPTER 19

I was thrilled with the new host. What a revelation! Living in Jenny's mind had been like living in a shipboard pool with none of the detail, the sensory appeal of a true Yeerk pool.

Allison fought me. What a glorious fight she made of it! I used to toy with her, withdraw some small bit of my control, just to see how long it would take her to find the weakness and attempt to exploit it.

Once I surrendered control of a single eye. Just my left eye, nothing more. Allison discovered that she could change the direction of that one eye. And here was her genius: She hid this ability, realized within a millisecond that to use it would be to betray it to me.

She waited. Waited. She knew she could do only one thing with that eye: Close it and eliminate my ability to perceive depth. She waited a week, till I was driving a car on a busy road, going at a high speed. I was driving behind a truck with defective brake lights.

Then, at the perfect moment, she closed her eye. Suddenly I could no longer be sure of the interval between me and the truck that was braking in front of me. I didn't know if it was stopping or maintaining speed.

I missed a fatal collision by milliseconds. She had been trying to kill herself, and me. Better dead than a Controller.

I was caught by surprise. I had not known that humans would do that. Die rather than accept defeat. Oh, I knew that they *said* they'd do it, but not that they would actually mean it.

It was a depressing insight. Victory always involves a certain amount of bluff. The weaker party must realize that he is weaker and be prepared to submit. A species that will not submit is useless. There was no profit in simply killing humans. We needed them alive. We are not predators, after all.

Fortunately, few humans are Allison Kim.

<You see that she does not even attempt to conceal her sympathies!> Visser Three's hated voice interrupted my memories. <She admires this human host.>

"Yes," I admitted, shaken back to the present. The present, in all its hopelessness. "You see, Visser Three, I intended to take the humans and make them our slaves. It was a large objective. It was worth spending time to understand, to assess. I did not doubt that we could slaughter humans; the question was, could we make them ours?"

<Humans possess simple projectile weapons armed with explosives, ranging from chemical ordnance to fusion weapons,> Visser Three lectured pedantically. <They do not have energy beam weapons, Quantum viruses, sensor shield technology, Zero-space travel . . . their fastest craft fly at speeds measured in multiples of the speed of sound. Their so-called spacecraft are devoid of weapons.>

"There are more than five billion of them, Visser," I shot back. "And you may deride their projectile weapons, but a nine-millimeter bullet will kill a Hork-Bajir host body quite effectively. And Taxxons or Gedds? A Taxxon can be killed with a can opener!"

<You see her fear! You see her cowardice!> Visser Three crowed.

"I intended to win, Visser, not to make brave noises and loud speeches. When I began the mission to Earth we might, with luck, have been able to assemble and land a force of fifty thousand Hork-Bajir and twenty thousand Taxxons on Earth. Five billion humans, each firing a single bullet, could have missed nearly a hundred percent of the time and still wiped us out!"

<We can terrify them into surrender!> Visser Three cried.

"Ignorant fool! Humans have fought thousands of wars. Thousands! We as a race have fought a mere handful. They run straight into the bullets, Visser Three, again and again. Did you know that? They attack against insane odds. They defend what can't be defended. Outnumbered, outgunned, surrounded, hopeless, they will still fight, fight, fight till they are each and every one dead. Something you might know if you stopped posturing long enough to learn something!"

I forced a derisive laugh. "It's ironic, Visser Three, that you, you of all Yeerks, you who rose to prominence by studying the Andalites when no one else would, have turned so stupid when it comes to dealing with humans."

Visser Three blinked his large Andalite eyes. He knew I'd made a point at his expense. He had no answer. I pressed home my point.

"You see, Visser, a human forced to fight can be brave to the point of madness. But they have weaknesses, too. Enough weaknesses. Enough that they can still be ours, if we are patient."

I felt Garoff's eyes on me. Watching. Considering. Him and the rest of the Council.

Was Garoff himself the Emperor? Was he the only judge that mattered here? Or was he just a mouthpiece for the real power?

"Let us grant that humans are complex," Garoff said. "That is not the issue at hand. The issue at hand is your decision to live as a human, and to fail to contact us for two years."

"They are the same matter, Garoff," I said. "It was easy enough to see the way to control a weakling like Jenny Lines. I needed to know how to defeat a strong human. Allison Kim was strong."

<She had human children! By her own admission!>

"I needed to understand my prey, and family is central to their world view."

<A lie,> Visser Three said bitterly. <I request a live memory dump. Visser One is obviously not worthy of trust. It is clear that she has concealed evidence. I will enter her memory and root out the truth!>

I wanted to scream. My hand clutched at a nonexistent Dracon weapon. It was the ultimate violation. It would make me no better than . . . than . . .

<Me?> my host mocked. <Yes, you'd feel what it's like to have someone else controlling your memory, prying into your secrets. You'd see what it's like to have a filthy Yeerk in your —>

<Idiot! Don't you realize that Visser Three would find out the truth about your son?>

That silenced her. But she was not my real problem.

Garoff nodded, floating in his gravity-neutral zone. "Visser One would have to agree to a live memory interface."

"To this treasonous incompetent buffoon rooting through my mind? Never! Council members, I —"

Garoff raised a hand, silencing me. "In exchange for agreeing, we, the Council, would offer you immunity for all secondary crimes. We only want the truth of the major charge, Edriss, the charge that you have delayed the invasion of Earth by incompetence or for reasons of sympathy with the host population. We have no interest in minor rule breaking. And the interface would be strictly confined to the time in question."

"You suggest I trust *him*?" I pointed at Visser Three.

"No, I do not. I will conduct the memory probe," Garoff said. "If you agree, Visser One."

There it was. I was trapped. If I refused, I was guilty. But a live memory interface? It would mean I could hide nothing. Nothing at all of that year. Garoff would be in my head.

Death now. Or death later.

No choice.

Technicians inserted probes through my host's skull. I felt the slight electricity as they found my stretched, membrane-thin body wrapped around Eva's brain.

I felt a single mind, a single consciousness touching mine. Garoff.

He did not roughly seize control. He insinuated himself. His voice alone, at first. He asked polite questions. But we both knew the power was all his.

"Tell me," he said.

"Yes," I answered.

<Hey, what is that sound?> Eva laughed. <Oh, I know. It's the jaws of a trap snapping shut.>

CHAPTER 20

Live Memory Transfer Protocol

"No, human, don't be a fool. The superstring theory is more correct than you think. You've simply failed to see the next step."

I spoke aloud to my host. I'd had her for six weeks at this point. I was driving her car. We were stuck in traffic. Typical human disorganization and chaos. I was heading for a scientific conference in a city called San Francisco. The subject was superstring theory, a simplistic precursor to what even we Yeerks refer to as Andalite Harmonic Theory.

"It's not an end, it's a beginning," I said.

Allison Kim pressed for an explanation. She was trapped, helpless, but she still cared about learning. It was something we shared in common. She wanted to understand. And if that meant being pleasant to me, she was willing to do so.

We spoke a great deal. About physics. History.

About biology. She was fascinated by Yeerk biology. I was fascinated by human history. All her memories were mine to command, to open or close as I chose. It wasn't necessary for me to converse with her. But I found it pleasant. Yes, it was pleasant.

Essam had found and taken the human Hildy Gervais. He was often away, passing as a true human. He was gaining tremendous experience. Insight. And I got the impression that he enjoyed his human occupation.

I was alone most of the time. Alone among humans. Far, far from any fellow Yeerk besides Essam. I knew that by now a death sentence had been issued for me. I knew that my only hope of survival was to bring the humans, gift wrapped, to the leadership of the Empire.

And yet, now, at a time when I should have been all energy and excitement and defined purpose, I felt loose, lost, drifting. Lazy. Unmotivated.

<It's L.A.,> Allison said. <It does that to everyone. Too much sun, too much easy living.>

"Nonsense," I said. "Your human pleasures mean nothing to me."

<And you have no pleasures of your own, do you? You Yeerks are all work and no play.>

"When we have taken Earth you will learn to live without distractions."

<You'll never take Earth.>

She was so definite. So confident. "No? And why not?"

<You think you know us. You know nothing. You've seen the world through the eyes of a defeated soldier and a junkie bimbo. You know nothing. We'll defeat you, Edriss.>

It was my nightmare, of course. The fear that I was missing something. Overlooking something. Humans were so different, one from the next. I had seen so small a sample.

Of course Allison knew some of this. She thought she was manipulating me. She thought she was being clever.

Yes, she —

Suddenly, sitting beside me in the car was Garoff. The garb of a Council member was gone. He was a Hork-Bajir, sitting calmly in the passenger seat of a Toyota Camry.

"Are you so sure she wasn't succeeding?" he asked me.

It was absurd! Insane! In my mind I was there, back there, years in the past. And here was a Hork-Bajir, a Council member!

My mind was reeling, swimming. Too many voices in my head.

"No, no. She never tricked me!"

"Let's go forward one month," he ordered, and my mind simply leaped the weeks and month.

Then, he was gone. Evaporated.

<Better focus, Edriss,> my host taunted. <Can't make another mistake. Visser Three is already warming up the torture chamber for you.>

Eva! She was seeing my memories. The intrusion of the probes had opened them to her. Garoff, Eva, both inside my head! Get out! Leave me alone!

<What's the matter, Edriss? Don't you enjoy irony?>

Ignore the host! She was in the present. Not here, not now in the past. She had nothing to do with me waiting impatiently for Essam to come home. Waiting for Hildy Gervais. Where was he? He was always late.

I walked to the balcony and looked out over the water. Malibu. Allison Kim could never have afforded this place, of course, but Essam and I had emptied Lowenstein's bank accounts before vaporizing him.

And why not live well? That was part of my bet with Allison.

"A bet?" Garoff asked, appearing in the middle of the room.

"Yes, a bet," I said. "She . . . my human host, she challenged me. Challenged my knowledge of humans. If I wanted to conquer humans I would have to get inside them, know them, not just the few I could infest."

Garoff shook his head, disbelieving. "You made a bargain with a host?"

"Not a bargain! I was using her. Using her to . . ."

"Right now, in this memory, you're worried about Essam. You want him to come home from his work. Why?"

"Why? I . . . I miss him."

"More than that. I see it clearly in your memory, although you never admitted it. Your host finds Essam's host attractive."

"Irrelevant. Humans are prone to all sorts of ridiculous emotions."

"Forward one month," Garoff ordered.

"Ah!" I yelled. The volleyball was heading toward me in a fast, flat arc. I ran, planted my feet in the sand, and stretched out my arms to slap the ball back upward.

"Go, Allison!" Hildy Gervais yelled.

All this played in my head as though I were there, back there on that beach, feeling the sun on my human flesh, feeling the excitement, feeling the adrenaline.

And at the very same moment I saw Garoff standing invisible to everyone but me, insubstantial yet real, among the three players on the other team. They looked through him, ran through him.

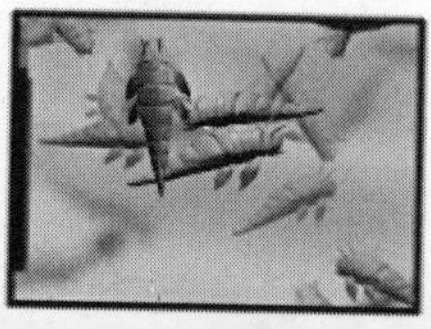

I knew what was coming next. Knew, and couldn't stop it from happening all over again.

The ball flew. A man on the other team slammed it back. Hildy ran for it. I ran for it. Slipped. Fell in the sand. Hildy fell atop me.

Face-to-face. Sudden silence. All the world outside was moving in slow motion.

I looked into his eyes. Knew that those eyes were being aimed by Essam. But knew, too, that Allison was looking at Hildy.

Yeerk looking at Yeerk. Human looking at human. None breathing. No heart beating.

Slowly, strangely reluctant, he pulled away.

I climbed up, brushed the sand from my lower back and legs.

Garoff stared at me, grim. "You experienced human emotions that were not derived from the host. It was you, Edriss, feeling a sort of exaggerated sympathy for Hildy, and for Essam within him."

<Can't be,> Eva whispered. <You were falling in love with him. You?>

"No, Council member, I was merely simulating human . . . human exaggerated sympathy . . . as a way to . . . to understand, Council Member Garoff. I never —"

"Forward one month!" he snapped.

Dinner. Candles. Lobster.

We were outdoors, on a veranda restaurant. The shadowed beach below us. The darkening ocean sighing beyond. Stars just beginning to twinkle into view.

Allison Kim loved lobster. Hildy Gervais loved crab. We were having both. Sharing bites across the table. Thinking nothing of it. But thinking of nothing else.

His fingers, holding out a white chunk of crab, dripping butter. I reach to take it with my own fingers, but it slips away.

He lifts another piece, places this one directly into my open mouth.

"She took you, Visser One," Garoff said contemptuously.

"No! No! All of it was part of learning, part of coming to understand humans. I had to know them to enslave them!"

"Forward. Six months."

"No, Garoff, there's nothing . . ."

"I see your memory as clearly as you do, Visser One. I see your memory as clearly as if you were my host body. I know what lies six months from this point."

"No," I whispered, helpless.

"I don't know if this will be good news or bad

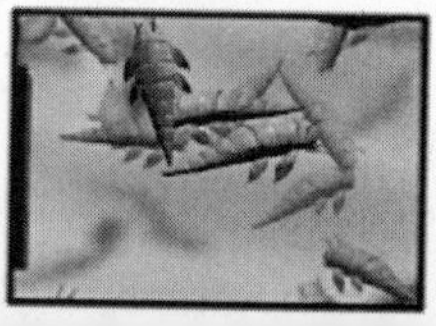

news, Allison," the doctor said. "But you're going to have twins."

She moved the primitive sonogram equipment over my swollen belly.

"Twins? You're sure?"

I looked at Hildy/Essam. He smiled.

"A little boy and a little girl. Twins."

Garoff walked through the doctor and looked down at me with furious Hork-Bajir eyes. "All a part of understanding humans, Edriss? All in service of the Yeerk Empire?"

From the bed, looking up helpless at him, I said, "No."

"No? You admit it?"

There was no point in lying. I had lied to myself then. Lied and told myself that I was simply investigating all aspects of human experience.

"Your host, this human, she turned you, Edriss."

"Yes. I . . . I was far, far from home. Far from the Empire. Sentenced to death for disobeying stupid orders. My host . . . her mind, her senses, she . . . she . . ."

"She what, Visser One of the Yeerk Empire? She *what*?"

"She was *alive*! She was alive! She was more alive than me. More alive than any of us."

Garoff nodded. "You had become Jenny Lines, Visser."

"What?" It didn't make any sense.

"You were addicted, Visser One. You became addicted to humans."

CHAPTER 21

"This is very troubling, Visser One," Garoff said.

"I am no traitor! I am not an Andalite sympathizer!"

"No. I don't think you are. But you are . . . or *were* . . . a traitor, Visser One. Memory forward three months."

I was in a bed. A narrow bed. I wore a simple pink robe. It was drenched with sweat. My hair was plastered down. My face was red from the strain of the previous four hours.

Essam/Hildy leaned over the bed, smiling. I smiled up at him, but only briefly. Then, I looked back down at the two very small faces. The boy, my son, had not opened his eyes, yet. But the girl, my daughter, blinked and looked up at me, her mind perfectly empty, receiving its first images. Images of me. Mother. Mommy.

Allison Kim. And a Yeerk named Edriss.

"What are we going to do?" Hildy/Essam whispered.

"I didn't know. I don't know."

"Allison, the shipboard Kandrona generators can not last much longer. We will need to replenish our supplies, if we are to survive."

I discovered I was crying when a tear dropped onto my son's face.

"I love you, Edriss," Essam, Essam *himself* said. "And I love these small humans. Our children."

Of course they weren't our children. They were the progeny of Allison and Hildy. These were infant humans, not Yeerks. Yeerks do not have any involvement with their progeny. Yeerk parents do not live to see their "children."

"What have we done?" he whispered.

"Signed our own death decrees," I said. "If we contact the Empire, and they learn of this, we will die. It won't matter what else we can tell them."

<The children must survive, Edriss,> Allison said inside my head. <You know that. You feel that. I know you do. You've come so far, learned so much. You know that the children, my children, and yes, your children, Edriss, they're what it's all about.>

"They will live," I whispered.

Essam/Hildy looked puzzled. Then he nodded. Essam and Hildy conferred within their shared brain. Then he said, "One thing we swear, the four of us, the children will survive."

"Stop," Garoff said. "Stop! Memory stop."

The memory disappeared. So sweet a memory, those small faces. So sweet a moment. The pain of it twisted my insides.

<I didn't know,> Eva said. <You never let me see that part of your past, Edriss. You loved them.>

"It was a powerful emotion, Garoff," I said. "I was not prepared. It had never been planned. Allison, my host, she never planned for things to go so far. Her plan was only to show me human happiness, human hope, human love. To weaken me, to make me see humans as more than mere host bodies. Things went too far. Essam was captured by the emotion of love."

"As were you, Visser One."

"I was . . . unprepared. Humans are complex. Gedds are barely sentient, Taxxons are mad beasts. Hork-Bajir, you take them, you see them from the start as intellectually inferior, primitive. You can tell yourself . . . you can shield yourself . . . but humans."

I was pleading. For what? Mercy? From a Council member of the Yeerk Empire?

"I was the first! We were the first, Essam and I. No one knew what humans held in their minds, no one knew. They weren't intellectual inferiors. They were impossible to dismiss as sub-Yeerk, not when you knew them."

Garoff nodded. He was in the room with me. Watching as I held the little girl to my breast. Watching with a mixture of disdain and worry on his Hork-Bajir face.

"I have learned all I need to know, Visser One. Terminate Live Memory Transfer Protocol."

I felt Garoff leave my mind.

Felt the probes being withdrawn.

It was all over. Over. My children . . . not mine, Allison's, but yes, mine, mine, too, mine! Lost!

Visser Three would unleash his war on Earth. The humans would resist. The violence would escalate. Out of control. The humans would lose every battle, every confrontation, and yet, they would fight on. And we, proud Yeerks, we could not let them survive to make fools of us.

I saw it all, as clearly as if it had already happened. Humans exterminated. Earth a blasted, blackened cinder. My children, my twins, my little ones . . .

I waited for the sound of Eva's crowing triumph. But she was silent.

The Council became visible again before my clearing vision. And Visser Three, waiting, tense, ready beside me.

All awaited Garoff's statement. For a long time he was silent, staring at nothing. Then, at last, he

shook his head and apologized. "I'm sorry to delay," he said. "We will now proceed with Visser One's statement."

I stared. What? *Continue?* From what point? Why? Why? I was convicted. I was guilty.

<There's another game being played here,> my host said. <Another game altogether.>

<No, no,> I argued. <He's just waiting . . . just . . .> But I didn't have an explanation. It was absurd! I wasn't an Andalite spy, but a traitor? Yes. Or had been.

<He's hoping for a way out,> Eva said. <You were not supposed to be convicted. They want a way out. You have to find it. You have to discredit Visser Three.>

"Marco," I whispered voicelessly.

<Yes. Marco. My child, to save yours.>

CHAPTER 22

"At . . . at what point shall I pick up the story, Council Member Garoff?" My voice was shaky, my hands trembling.

"At the point where I terminated direct memory contact, Visser One. Of course. Begin by telling us what became of the human progeny of your host and the host of your subordinate, Essam."

<Yes, tell us that, Visser One,> Visser Three agreed. <We would all be interested in that answer.>

I was lost. Confused. My human stomach was twisting. Head swimming. "I . . . the progeny, the humans?"

<The truth, Edriss. Tell me quickly!>

What? My host was now making demands? Impossible!

<I'll help, Yeerk, but tell me the truth!>

<Visser One seems unsure of which lie to tell next,> Visser Three said.

<They're free! But I can't tell *them* that! I have to say that I killed them!>

<No!> Eva shouted. <Visser Three is too eager. He can barely contain himself. What if Visser Three has them? What if he has your kids?>

I was stunned. I hadn't thought of that. Of course! First force me to confess to procreating as a human, then catch me lying to protect the children . . .

"The human progeny, the children, were given to other humans to raise," I said. "I terminated contact."

I felt Visser Three slump beside me. Just the slightest movement. But Eva had been right: Visser Three had them!

"And the host human, this Allison Kim?" Garoff asked. "Tell us what happened to her. Pick up the narrative, Visser One."

"Yes, Council Member Garoff. Only . . ."

"What?"

"This body, this human host requires some moments to perform necessary biological functions. Waste elimination and replacement of fluids and food."

<She doesn't need food!> Visser Three roared, completely forgetting his place. <Let us have the results of Garoff's investigation, let's end this farce and get on with the demands of justice! She doesn't

need food! She needs to be executed! She doesn't need FOOD!>

"Perhaps not," Garoff said blandly. "But Hork-Bajir, too, need food, Visser Three. With the concurrence of my fellow Council members? Yes? We will adjourn for one standard hour."

The hologram went blank.

I was in the room, surrounded by Hork-Bajir, and faced with Visser Three.

<Aaaarrrgghhh!> Visser Three screamed and slammed his tail blade into the wall.

"You really should learn some self-control, Visser."

We stared at each other. Hatred, pure and undiluted.

<Take her to the feeding building for human-Controllers,> Visser Three ordered the Hork-Bajir. <I do not need to remind you that if she so much as thinks of escape, you will each be killed.>

I stood up, slowly, awkwardly. My injuries had made me old. "I don't think I'll be running very far, Visser," I said wearily.

Visser Three walked behind me as I shuffled down the hallway. The Hork-Bajir guards flanked me, left and right, jostling me as I went.

Then, we stepped out into the main Yeerk pool. It was a vast, domed, underground space. The floor and walls were mostly still bare dirt. The arched roof

was supported in part by steel beams, but was still mostly just so much dirt held in place by force fields.

A number of structures surrounded the pool itself: the various temporary housing facilities, the feeding sheds of the Taxxons, and storage warehouses. Two long, steel piers extended out into the pool. One was used for Yeerks leaving their hosts, the other for Yeerks returning.

There were cages, of course, for the temporarily freed hosts. The hosts often cried or shouted. Pointless, of course. They could not escape.

The cafeteria for humans was a long, narrow tin-and-plywood structure. It was filled with noisy human-Controllers eating and talking.

Our appearance killed the conversation.

Room was made for me. I sat on one of the benches. The service Gedd came hustling over with a plate. Grilled chicken, boiled potatoes, steamed broccoli. The Yeerks who ran the facility stayed current on human nutritional needs.

I sat. A Hork-Bajir guard sat on either side of me. Visser Three watched as I ate.

Across from me the human-Controllers kept their eyes on their plates and ate with mechanical speed. No one was interested in making small talk with me. At the same time, no one wanted to insult me by leaving.

I was a pariah. Unless I wasn't. I was a loser. Unless it turned out that I was a winner. I almost felt sorry for my brother Yeerks. So hard for them to tell which Visser to obey today.

I needed an opening. Just a small one. Anything.

But there was nothing. Hork-Bajir everywhere. Visser Three himself almost breathing down the back of my neck.

I had to push. I had to create an opening.

"Deeedly-deet. Deeedly-deet. Deeedly-deet."

Someone's cell phone ringing. A person three places down on my same side of the table. A human woman.

She smiled nervously. "It's . . . it's necessary for my cover," she explained to Visser Three, to me, to Visser Three, her eyes darting back and forth.

<Then answer it!> Visser Three snapped.

"Hello?" A pause. "Yes, sir. I'm en route to the client now, but I'm tied up in traffic."

Cell phone. It worked from here? From this far underground? They must have installed transponders to allow Yeerks to stay in touch while passing through.

Cell phone. If I could take that phone. If I could . . .

But how? One wrong move and Visser Three would have me cut apart.

No. No, wait. He wouldn't. *Couldn't*. Oh, he'd stop me, but he couldn't kill me. Not now, now that

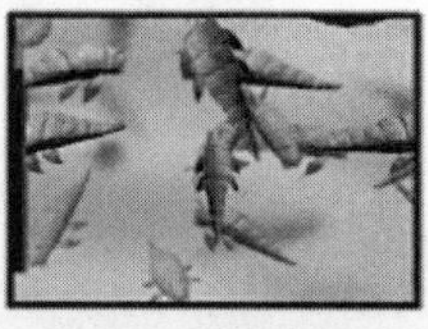

he was under suspicion himself. It would look to the Council as if he was trying to protect himself by killing his accuser.

I had one good hand, fingers still fairly limber. Was it enough? Would I have the strength, the finesse?

I finished eating, watching the woman out of the corner of my eye. She pushed her plate away. I stood up.

"I'm done."

She stood up. Both moving, Hork-Bajir standing up, moving back, Visser Three backpedaling to make way for me, the woman moving toward me, saw her mistake, saw she'll run into me, stopped, too late, I stumbled, tripped on my wrecked feet, fell into her.

Down she went! Me on top. I cursed, annoyed. Like the visser I am.

"Clumsy idiot!"

Hork-Bajir rushed to grab me, picked me up. The woman tried to help, pushed me up, but politely. Not angry, just wanting no part, even indirect, in this civil war between vissers.

A Hork-Bajir grabbed me and yanked me straight up. The pain in my shoulder was shocking, like an electric shock.

But I had the cell phone.

CHAPTER 23

Toilet facilities. Not very elegant, but very clean. They were cleaned every twenty minutes by Gedds. We didn't want to be transmitting human viruses back and forth, after all, and reduce the efficiency of our human hosts.

In the toilet, the door closed, the tiny building ringed by Hork-Bajir, I dialed the number.

Ring. Ring.

My heart was in my throat. My emotions. Eva's emotions. Nothing clear in this moment of desperation. All insanity! Madness! I was calling my enemy for help against a creature who should be an ally. I was using my host's child to save my own.

Ring. Ring.

Answer! Answer, damn you! Answer!

"Hi, we're not at home, or maybe we just don't feel like answering the phone, so leave a message, you know the drill."

Answering machine. His voice. All over. All over.

Beep!

<Take the chance, Yeerk! You have no choice!>

"Mar . . ." My throat was dry. I took a breath. "Marco, if you're there, pick up."

Click.

I breathed again.

"What?" he asked, carefully masking the fear, the despair, he must be feeling. Visser One was calling him. Visser One *knew*! He must be seeing the end now, feeling the hopelessness of final defeat.

I got some small pleasure from that.

"You know who this is," I whispered.

"Yes."

"Your mother."

"No," he said flatly. "*Not* my mother. A Yeerk."

"Okay. Granted. But she needs you. She needs you and your friends."

"My friends?"

"Don't play stupid, Marco. I know you. What you *are*. What you *do*. You are needed. Now. As quickly as you can. You need to be seen."

"By who?"

"Visser Three."

Silence.

"It's not a trap!" I whispered urgently.

"I know. Like you said, you know me. If you wanted me dead it would be easy. You could take me, infest me, and have all of my friends within a few hours. So you *need* me. This is about your little personality conflict with Visser Three. You're desperate. But you won't give me up to Visser Three because you hate him more than you hate us."

I almost choked. From almost no information he had painted a very cogent picture of the situation.

Then I almost laughed. "I once thought you were too soft, too gentle."

"Yeah, well, things change."

<You've had enough time in there!> Visser Three said from outside the toilet.

"Marco, I'm out of time!" I hissed. "Will you do it?"

"Where?"

"The pool."

"Forget it. Too tough a target, Visser."

"It's your mother's life on the line, he'll kill her, too! He'll use her to torture me."

"The Yeerk pool is too secure," Marco said calmly.

My mind was racing. Incredible! The little monster was cold-bloodedly writing off his own mother!

"They . . . they deliver fresh meat for the Taxxons later today. This evening, I guess. In an hour and a half! Comes in by transport ship. They open the dome ingress."

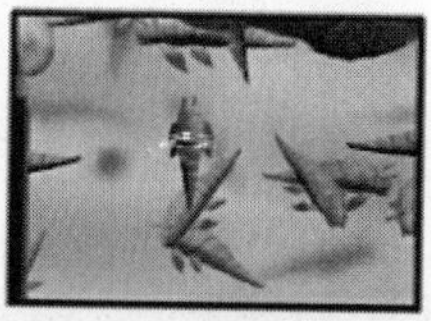

He hesitated.

<Visser One, get out of there or I will have you dragged out!> Visser Three roared.

"Where's the dome opening nowadays?" Marco asked laconically. "I think we kind of messed up the last one."

I told him in quick, spare detail. Then, "You'll do it?"

He didn't answer. Instead he said, "Mom, I know you can hear me. I don't know if I can save you. You understand that, right? I'll do what's right. I'll do what I have to do."

It was his only show of emotion. His voice cracked when he said "Mom."

<I know you will. I love you,> Eva said, silent, a prisoner inside her own skull.

"Marco, your mother loves you," I said.

But if I'd been expecting him to soften, I got the opposite result.

"I know my mother loves me, Visser," he said. "And let me make one thing clear: There's no deal between us, you and me, Yeerk. I'll kill you for what you've done to her and to my dad. Count on that."

He hung up.

The door burst in as I slammed the cell phone into the toilet bowl and flushed.

Preposterous! A scrawny teenager threatening

me. I was a prisoner of Visser Three, already all but condemned to a death by torture and starvation. Did the child think he could frighten me? It was laughable.

<And yet you're not laughing, are you, Yeerk?>

CHAPTER 24

They kept me waiting for almost an hour. I could only imagine what was happening among the Thirteen. Maybe they were dealing with some entirely unrelated matter. Perhaps the strange disappearance of the task force that had been sent to investigate the Anati planet.

But more likely they were debating my fate. Deciding if I would live or die. Or, if I was to die, how and when.

At last, when I felt I couldn't stand the suspense any longer, the hologram reappeared.

Garoff spoke. "Now, Visser One, you may resume your narrative. You were about to tell us what happened to the host Allison Kim."

"Yes. Yes, I was."

I was telling a story that was suicide to tell. My deadliest enemy was my prosecutor. My judge, one of them at least, was motivated by some impulse I could not fathom. And I had just called on a group of Andalites and morph-capable humans to attack my own people.

I was crippled with pain, weak, surrounded. Visser Three; Garoff; my host's child, Marco. Any of the three might kill me. And all I could do was talk.

"Essam and I needed a supply of Kandrona. The shipboard Kandrona was weakening. It should have been able to last another year, at least. But it was running low. We would starve. And that would mean the end of the mission."

<So, at last, after more than a year of passing as a human, procreating as a human, you decided to contact the Empire!> Visser Three said. He laughed. <How dutiful of you.>

"I contacted the Empire. They threatened me, of course. I had stolen a ship and disappeared. But then I said the magic words: Class-Five species."

Even now, even here in this terrible situation, I savored the memory. "It was a sub-visser Ninety-two I spoke with first. 'I have located a Class-Five species,' I told him. 'A Class-Five species with superior dexterity and above average sensory capabilities.'

"'Numbers?' the sub-visser demanded.

"'Five billion. Give or take.'

"I remember the way the sub-visser sat bolt upright. I believe he cut himself with his own Hork-Bajir blades.

"He repeated it back, cautiously. 'You mean five million, Sub-Visser?'

"'No, Sub-Visser,' I said. 'I mean five billion. As in five thousand millions.'

"I explained my concept for The Sharing and sent him a recording I had made of the very first voluntary human host. I outlined my plan for an invasion of Earth that would not require us to strip our forces from the rest of the galaxy, an invasion that would require a relative handful of Yeerks. After that, naturally, there was no more discussion of arresting me.

"I went home from that contact elated and found Essam/Hildy caring for the children. They were infants, of course. He was changing their diapers. I told him, casually, that a new Kandrona was on the way. He became irrational. Emotional."

"What was the cause of his irrationality?" Garoff asked.

"He said I should not have contacted the Empire. We could, according to him, fly our ship back to Yeerk space, invent some story of being lost, and obtain a new Kandrona generator before returning to Earth. He'd wanted to talk to me about it. He was angry that I'd gone, on my own, to make contact."

<She's trying to blame a dead Yeerk for her own treason!> Visser Three cried.

"I contacted the Empire!" I yelled in his face. "If I'd wanted to —"

<Months had gone by!>

"I had used the time to understand humans. To learn their strengths and weaknesses. I had already started The Sharing. I was a spy, Visser Three. A secret agent working undercover. It was me and Essam, alone. What did you expect me to do? Use our one ship to attack the White House?"

"A spy," Garoff said thoughtfully. "Yes, a spy would want to blend in with the surrounding world. Might even need to simulate a certain sympathy with the local populace."

I saw Visser Three's tail twitch. A gesture of surprise. Garoff had just shown his hand: Garoff was on my side. Garoff had performed the live memory interface, and now he was defending me, however indirectly.

I enjoyed that moment. I enjoyed the frisson of fear that traveled along Visser Three's Andalite spine.

"Continue with the narrative," Garoff said.

"Yes, Council member."

I adjusted my damaged arm, easing the pain just a bit. "Essam became irrational, as I said. But I was able to convince him of the necessity and rightness of my actions. So I believed, anyway. I told him the children were irrelevant. We were Yeerk officers,

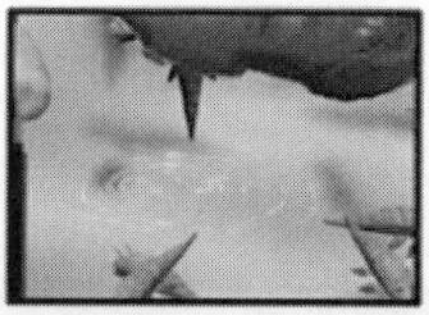

representatives of the Empire, we had a duty, we had a joyful duty."

<That's laying it on a little thick,> Eva said. <Go with blunt and honest. I'm guessing they don't get a lot of that.>

Now my host was giving advice. Helping. Trying to save me. It was the ultimate humiliation.

"And what did Essam reply?" Garoff asked.

"He said, 'Yes, you're right, of course.' And I, for my part, continued to cajole and reason and explain. I still needed Essam's assistance, if I could get it. I told him I understood his concerns. And yes, I freely admit that the long time alone, cut off, and living as a human without the counterbalance of Yeerk companionship, had drawn me into an unprofessional sympathy with humans. With my host. And, through her, with the progeny, the children."

<That's it. Smart. Admit what's obvious anyway.>

"But my emotional sympathies did not obscure my duty. I knew where that lay. I knew that this Class-Five species was a vital natural resource. I assumed that Essam would see all that, too. I did not see that Essam was weaker than I. We all know that Essam had risen at one point in his career to subvisser rank and had been demoted for improper behavior. Specifically, a lack of vigor. A lack of firmness. I thought Essam understood and agreed with me. I was wrong."

<Very nice, Yeerk,> Eva said. <You've dovetailed it all nicely with what Garoff saw in your memories. You had human sympathies, but you overcame them. How noble.>

"We had relocated from Hollywood. I'd concluded that Hollywood was not the best place for an invasion I knew would have to go unnoticed for some years. Hollywood is watched. And Hollywood was already saturated with movements bearing a superficial similarity to my concept for The Sharing. So we moved away, to a place where The Sharing would have less competition for the credulous.

"It was easy to find a new job for Allison. But my life was becoming more complicated. I had by this time begun The Sharing, and I was using a second host, part-time, for that task. I was constantly running from Allison's job to Sharing-related business, with a change of hosts between each. Very time-consuming."

"Where are you going, Essam?" I demanded.

"Don't worry, I'll leave you the Kandrona," he said. "I won't starve you. I . . . I actually thought I loved you. And for that I'll not hurt you now."

"What are you babbling about?"

"I've just fed. I'll last three days. I'll release Hildy at that point. He'll be safe with the children by then."

"You think you're leaving?" I cried.

"Yes, Allison, I —"

"I am Sub-Visser Four-hundred-nine, not 'Allison'!" I roared.

"Yes, Sub-Visser," Essam said. "But I am no longer a member of the Empire. I have chosen death over a continuation of this despicable mission."

CHAPTER 25

I could not believe my ears, Council members. I was shocked. Stunned. I tried to understand.

"Despicable? Have you gone mad, Essam? We are Yeerks!"

"Yes, we are. But we will have to find a better way than this," Essam said.

I was in a rage. Betrayed! Betrayed by my own . . . by my subordinate! By Hildy, by Essam, betrayed! I ran for the hidden panel where we concealed the weapons.

I reached in, grabbed one of the Dracon weapons, turned, and leveled it at Essam.

"Obey me or die now," I snapped.

"If you fire you may hit the children."

"Do you think I care? Obey me! I am your subvisser!"

He put the children down and moved away from them. "Kill me then, Edriss."

I ordered my finger to squeeze the trigger. But at that moment my host rose up against me. She had

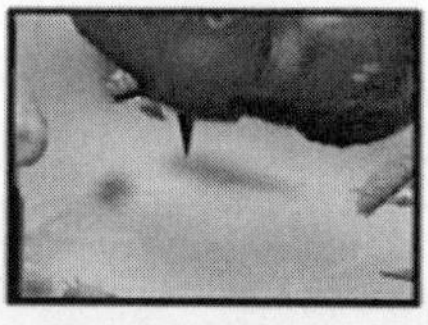

lain in wait, biding her time, lulling me into a false sense of security. She attacked with all the force of mind she possessed. Naturally I regained control within seconds. But in those few seconds Essam leaped and snatched the Dracon beam away from me.

<That's a nice story, Yeerk. Is any of it true?>

<I couldn't let him take my children. I told him, "Stop worrying, you fool, I can keep the children safe. They'll be ours. I'll be a full visser, don't you see? I'll be able to protect them.">

<He didn't believe you.>

<He believed me.>

<Then why?>

<It went beyond the children, can't you see that? He was in love.>

<With whom?>

<Allison Kim . . . his own host, Hildy Gervais . . . Humans. He was in love with it all. He was in love with love. He had gone over. He had become human, in some way.>

<And he chose to die rather than surrender his humanity,> Eva said. <And still, you think you will conquer us?>

Garoff cleared his throat. "Visser One?"

"Sorry, Council Member. I . . . never mind. Essam was . . . was larger than me, stronger, being in a male human host. He held me prisoner. He knew my feeding schedule. He held me against my will, waiting till I was starving. At last I had no choice: I prepared to enter our temporary pool.

"'The children will need their mother,' Essam said.

"'I *am* their mother!' I cried, a lie of course, but I hoped to manipulate him.

"'No. Allison Kim is their mother. You? You are no one's mother. You never could be.'

"'You've gone *human*, you fool!'

"He smiled. 'Yes, I have "gone human," Sub-Visser.'

"'What will you do, traitor?' I demanded. 'Will you leave me in this pool with no host? Leave me here trapped, eventually discovered, flushed down the toilet by whatever human comes to investigate the disappearance of Allison Kim?'

"He was troubled. He was reluctant. But at the end he agreed to lock my alternate host onto the poolside restraints. I had acquired a large, impressive male for use in speaking to my Sharing groups. This alternate host spent his days in a padlocked, soundproof room.

"He brought me the second host, attached him using the restraining devices Essam himself had built, and left. I immediately entered this host and

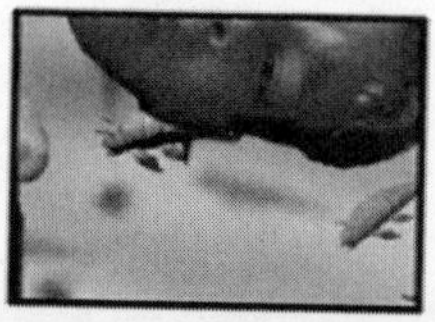

went in search of Essam and Allison Kim and the children."

"Why did you follow Essam?" Garoff asked.

"To kill him, of course."

<Liar. You loved him.>

"And the children?" Garoff asked.

"They were irrelevant," I said flatly.

<And you love them still, Yeerk.>

"I had created the children in an attempt to learn about humans. I had become attached to them, yes. Or at least my host had. And, as I said, I had become . . . confused. But now that I was free of Allison Kim, my mind was clear once more. There was no need to destroy the children; they were infants and knew nothing. Destroying them would have involved risk for no gain. I knew that humans would adopt them and solve my problem."

"Logical," Garoff commented.

Visser Three was having none of that. <Does this traitor expect us to believe that she gave live birth to humans so that she could "learn" about humans? We have thousands of human-Controllers who pass quite well without procreating!>

"You've never understood anything but brute force and crude manipulation, Visser Three. Your plans are grandiose and absurd. You wasted how much time and how many resources inventing a clever potion to destroy human free will? A failure! As anyone who knows humans could have told you. You try and seize control of the heads of state of the most powerful nations and end up alarming them, making half of them suspect our presence on Earth! You spend a fortune in pursuit of an Anti-Morphing Ray that doesn't work! Why? Because you cannot even manage to wipe out a handful of Andalite refugees!"

<You forget, Visser One, I *have* wiped out the Andalite bandits.>

"Yes, I had forgotten that little demonstration," I said with a derisive sneer. "Congratulations. You lost how many valuable Hork-Bajir hosts in the process over these many months? How many Yeerks killed?"

<The mistake was following the path laid down by you, Visser One. You and your Sharing, your one-host-at-a-time, your slow, steady infiltration. We *took* the Gedds. We *took* the Hork-Bajir!> He made a fist with his weak Andalite hand. <*Took* them! We made allies of the Taxxons, but if they had resisted, we would have taken them, too!>

He strode back and forth before the hologram, practically prancing in the excitement of hearing his own ranting.

<Do you think we will infiltrate the Andalites

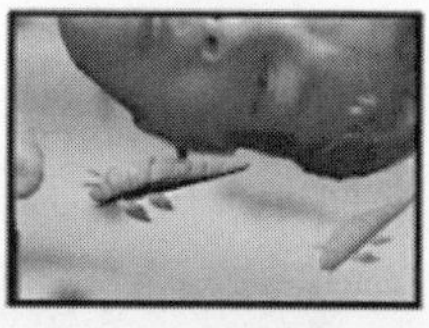

when that time comes? Will we form little social clubs and talk them into becoming our slaves? No! When we are ready we will *take* them, too!>

He stopped moving and turned all four of his eyes on me. <We are the Yeerk Empire! We are not a race of sneaks and spies. We are rulers, conquerors!>

The speech had an effect. I saw several of the Council members standing taller in their gravity-neutral field, squaring shoulders and jutting their jaws. They were, after all, politicians and thus easily swayed by grand visions.

I waited till the echoes of Visser Three's thought-speak faded. Then I said, "You know, I was wrong about Visser Three, he's not a dupe of the Andalites. Rather, with all this bluster and raving he sounds as if he's been spending his time with Helmacrons."

There was a bark of laughter from some member of the Council. The Helmacrons were the tiniest sentient species known, barely bigger than a grain of sand, but with enormous egos.

Visser Three ignored the laughter. <It's very simple, Visser One: You pushed the policy of slow infiltration for one reason, and one reason only: You feared a war of conquest would destroy your children.>

<Careful! It's a trap!>

"Nonsense!" I cried. "I care nothing for the human children! Nothing!"

Visser Three smiled an Andalite smile, and I felt a sinking sensation. My host had seen it. I had not. Yes, a trap.

<As it happens, Council Members, this is my day for surprises,> Visser Three said. <Bring him in.>

The door opened.

The child walked in. He would be nine years old now.

I had last seen him years ago. For a long time, whenever I'd been on Earth, I had followed their progress, my twins, my babies.

This was my son. His name was Darwin. That had been a little joke on my part. He represented something never evolved: a human child with four parents, two human, two Yeerk.

<I'm afraid I can't trust you with a Dracon beam, Visser,> my enemy said. <But as you pointed out, human projectile weapons are quite effective.>

One of the Hork-Bajir produced a human handgun. I took it. No choice. My hand was sweating, my heart . . . no! Not this!

<A single bullet, Visser One. Show us. Prove to us that you care nothing for this human child.>

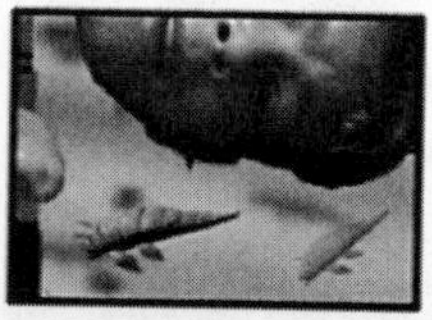

CHAPTER 26

I held the gun.

And Darwin, my son, calmly took the barrel in his right hand and pressed the muzzle against his own heart.

I understood. Darwin was a Controller. The Yeerk inside his brain was holding the gun so that I couldn't spin around and shoot Visser Three. Holding the gun so that the only person I could kill was Darwin.

The Yeerk's host body would die, my son would die. The Yeerk might be rescued in time. It was dangerous for him, though. Visser Three must have threatened him terribly to get him to do this.

I looked at my son, the features that were a unique blend of Allison's Korean and Hildy's French physiology. The eyes, the hair, were Allison's. The skin was pale, the mouth wide, all Hildy's.

Nothing of me, of course. How could there be? And yet, this child would not have existed but for me. Surely that made me in some part his mother.

I struggled to control my facial expression. I was helped by the injuries. I had seen myself in the mirror; my right eye always seemed to be crying now.

Darwin a Controller. His sister? My daughter? Where was Madra? Where was my little girl, named for the bright, tiny moon of the Yeerk home world?

The gun was trembling in my hand. Pull the trigger. It was all I had to do. I would be free. Visser Three had staked everything on this one showdown.

If I refused I would be beyond even Garoff's power to save.

<Perhaps Visser One is unfamiliar with the operation of the weapon,> Visser Three smirked. <That seems unlikely in the extreme, but just to refresh her memory, you pull the trigger, Visser. Just pull the trigger!>

<You can't do this, Edriss,> Eva said.

<I have no choice! They'll kill me!>

<Once before you chose your life over love. Are you happy with the result?>

<Simply squeeze, Visser. Then . . . bang! And the lead projectile tears a hole through — >

"Will you fire or not?" Garoff demanded. He was trapped now, as well. He could do nothing to save me. He could only hope I would fire.

Strange how much Darwin looked like her. Like Allison. Strange, too, how much I thought I could

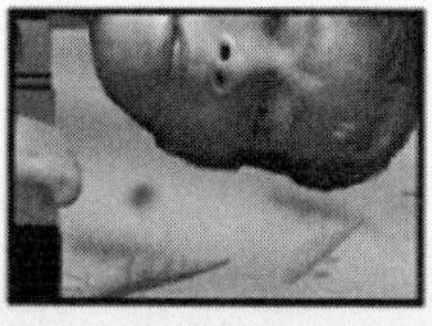

see something, something, some small thing in his eyes that was from me.

I had to do it.

Had to.

Garoff staring. The Council all rapt. All four of Visser Three's Andalite eyes on me, straining. Even the Hork-Bajir guards were staring holes through me.

Only I was looking beyond. Only I could really see.

"No choice," I whispered.

I tightened my finger on the trigger.

Stall. Delay. A few more seconds. A few more seconds and the flea, the tiny insect, would be done growing.

I smiled at Visser Three. "You lose, Visser. You have misjudged me. I will kill this human grub and then, in my own good time, I will see you die the torture death of a traitor!"

<Fire, then! Fire!>

"I hope this is a hollow-point slug, Visser Three. It would be a waste if the slug should pass through and kill the Hork-Bajir-Controller standing behind him."

<FIRE!>

Visser Three's host body was no longer the only Andalite in the room.

FWAPP!

FWAPP!

The young Andalite struck with lightning speed! Two Hork-Bajir dropped, each having failed to stand on a single remaining leg.

<Now!> the young Andalite yelled.

WHAM!

The door blew inward. A flash of orange and black, teeth and claws and dazzling speed, exploded into the room. A split second later there came a rolling, rumbling mass of shaggy off-white fur, large as a small truck.

The Hork-Bajir tripped into each other in their eagerness to attack. But now two new creatures were with us, two Hork-Bajir.

The two morphed Hork-Bajir dived in amid the massed Hork-Bajir guards, sowing confusion and hesitation.

It all happened in a second. A second to go from Visser Three's frustrated roar to utter mayhem.

<No!> Visser Three cried.

Darwin released his grip on the gun barrel.

I swung the gun toward the polar bear and fired. The bullet hit. But if the polar bear even noticed, it showed no sign.

"HHHUUHHHRRROOOOAAARR!"

Hork-Bajir-Controllers were down, left and right.

One drew his Dracon weapon and fired.

TSEEEEW!

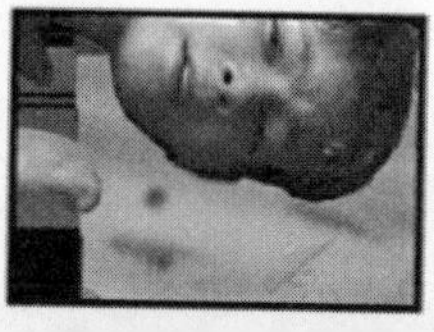

WHOOOSH!

"Aaaahhhh!"

Backflash! The energy beam missed its target, burned into the rock wall and exploded in heat energy. Visser Three's blue Andalite fur crinkled and curled up black from the heat.

<Fool! No weapons!> Visser Three ordered.

Visser Three was in the battle, formidable as always in direct combat. But half the Hork-Bajir guards were already down, injured or worse. And from second to second in the melee it was impossible to tell our Hork-Bajir from theirs.

<Every Yeerk within the sound of my voice, to me!> Visser Three bellowed.

Reinforcements would be quick in coming. There were dozens of Hork-Bajir-Controllers within the Yeerk pool complex, and numerous Taxxons, as well.

"Andalite filth!" Darwin took a futile swing at the young Andalite and got the flat of a tail blade against his head in return. He went down, unconscious. Not dead! Safe! A Hork-Bajir talon stepped on his back. That would bruise but not cause permanent harm.

The tiger and the polar bear were everywhere, slashing, roaring till I felt my ears would bleed. I crouched in a corner, hands over my ears, cowering, afraid, stunned at the concentrated violence. I was helpless amid all these claws and teeth and talons and slashing blades. Human fingers were nothing without a weapon to hold.

<Behind you!> one of the morphed Hork-Bajir yelled.

The tiger spun, slashed, hissed, slashed again, all in the time a human eye might blink. A Hork-Bajir staggered back, holding his own internal organs in his hands.

It was uncontrolled mayhem, a dozen combatants still standing, all crammed into a single room, no one running, not yet. Madness all around me!

The polar bear slammed a pile-driver shoulder into Visser Three's side and sent him sprawling. But the visser was quick, with all the formidable physical prowess of a mature Andalite.

He leaped toward the young Andalite. Face-to-face, they tail fought, fencers whipping their blades at a speed that cracked the air.

I saw the Council, hovering safe in their hologram. Again they were spectators at a battle. Like human fans at a sporting event. They called out advice, groaned at defeat, cheered at victory. One of the Taxxon Council members became so excited he ate the head of a passing Gedd attendant in a single bite of his red-rimmed mouth.

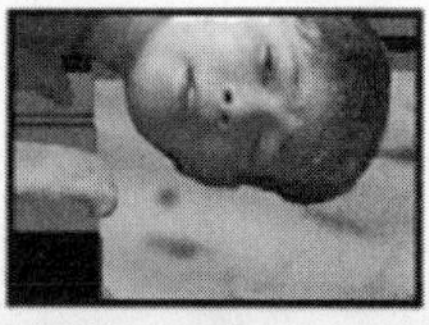

Now the Council saw the truth: *This* was what it meant to fight the so-called Andalite bandits. Not the ludicrous shadow play Visser Three had staged earlier.

This was the reality.

I was almost afraid it would excite sympathy for Visser Three. Now the Council members saw for themselves what a handful of morph-capable warriors could do.

But no, no, it was too late for Visser Three now. He had lied to the Council. Worse yet, he had treated them like fools. And now he had been caught in that lie.

Visser Three slashed for the tiger, a blow no human could avoid. But the tiger jerked its eager, quizzical face back and swiped with claws that barely missed ripping open the visser's chest.

<Reinforcements! Every Yeerk within the sound of my voice!> Visser Three screamed. He was beginning to realize that he might be killed, right here, right now, with the entire Council watching.

But the next creature through the door was neither Hork-Bajir nor Taxxon.

It was a gorilla.

<So,> Marco said to me. <Was this what you had in mind?>

I nodded slightly.

The gorilla, without turning its eyes away from me, slammed a cinder-block fist into the face of a Hork-Bajir guard.

Then he knuckle-walked over to me. He drew back his fist and, a split second later, everything went black.

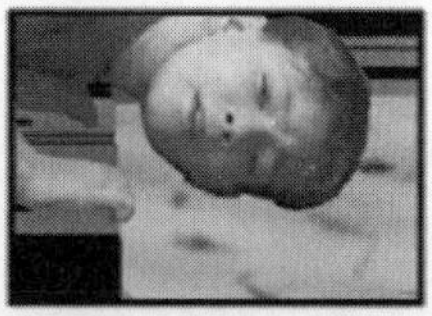

CHAPTER 27

I woke to pain.

Eyes open. My nose flattened. I touched it with my good hand then looked at my fingers. Blood, just starting to clot, not yet dry. So I hadn't been out for long.

I was in a small, dimly lit tunnel or cave. It took me a few minutes to figure it out. Then I realized I was in a Taxxon tunnel. The Taxxons had made several branching off from the main pool.

A dead, deflated-looking Taxxon lay twenty feet away down the tunnel, guts spilled and stinking.

I turned, looked over my shoulder, and got a terrible shock.

The Yeerk pool complex was plainly visible. Not fifty yards away heavily armed Hork-Bajir were racing here and there, looking, there was no doubt, for me. For us.

And yet, despite the fact that we should have been in plain sight, they did not see us.

Evidently we were behind a hologram. I did not

see any sort of hologram generator. But then there was no reason the hologram generator couldn't conceal itself. One of the rocks might be the generator.

The tiger, the polar bear, the two Hork-Bajir, and the young Andalite surrounded me, staying at a cautious distance. They were nervous, but not showing it too much.

Marco sat on his haunches, human now, wearing bike shorts and a T-shirt. He watched me, his expression unreadable.

"You need to see a doctor, Visser. That damage wasn't all my doing."

"Visser Three," I whispered through broken teeth. "Did you kill him?"

Marco shook his head. "No. He morphed. We took off."

"Pity," I said. "They'll find you here."

"We know. But not just yet."

"You have very sophisticated holographic capabilities, it would seem. Better than anything we Yeerks possess." I narrowed my eyes. "Better, perhaps, than Andalites possess."

"Just a little something we put together from stuff we bought at Radio Shack," Marco said. "Now. Why are we here?"

"You've served your purpose," I said. "You can go."

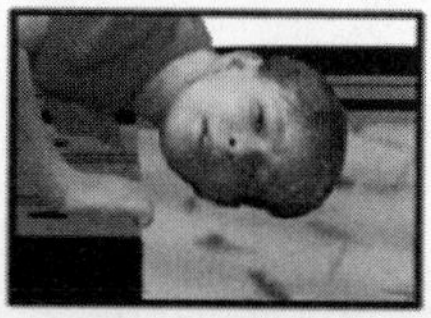

He nodded. "So we were just supposed to put in an appearance."

"Exactly."

"Interesting little war you Yeerks are carrying on. Are you sure you know who you're fighting?"

I laughed. "I know everything, now."

<You think you'll scare him, Edriss? You don't yet grasp what is right before your eyes.>

Marco seemed to echo his mother's confidence. "Don't waste your time trying to scare me, Visser One. If we ever get taken prisoner some Yeerk will have full access to my memory, everyone's memory, here. That phone call you made? Please come kick butt on my fellow Yeerks? That'll be known to your brother and sister Yeerks."

<He sees it,> Eva said. <He sees the trap you're in.>

<The boy is clever,> I admitted. <He has grown.>

<You infested me at random, so you believe. But I believe in higher powers, Yeerk. I believe I was taken so that my son would grow strong and wise and some day destroy you.>

"Yes, that may all be true, Marco," I said. "But if you are dead you'll talk to no one."

Marco bit his lip. Looked down at the ground. "Ax?" he said.

The young Andalite's tail blade was at my throat before I could blink.

"Here's the deal, Yeerk. You leave my mother. You do it right now. We'll throw you into the pool. Let you live a bit longer."

"Or?"

"Or my Andalite friend here twitches."

"You won't do it. You're looking at your mother's face. Her eyes. You can't. You're just a human, with all the usual human weaknesses."

Marco stood up, but even standing he was only a little taller than me, sitting. "You know what it says on the New Hampshire license plates?"

I shook my head in confusion.

"Access the memories," he said. "My mom knows. We talked about it. At the time we thought it was kind of corny. But then, the more we thought about it, it wasn't corny at all. It was . . . inevitable."

I accessed the memories. "Live free or die?"

"Live free or die," Marco echoed. "My mother walks out of here a free woman, or she dies."

<He doesn't mean it!> I told Eva.

<Yes. He does. You have to let me talk to him. Me, without you. Me alone.>

"Ten seconds," Marco said. "Ticktock. Ten . . . nine . . . eight . . ."

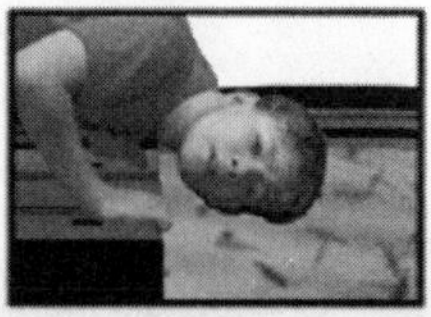

CHAPTER 28

<No! Do you think I'm a fool?>

<You don't have a choice, Edriss.>

<I can still choose between types of death, human. Do you think I will trust your vile, cold-blooded son there? He's sworn to kill me!>

"Six . . . five . . ."

<He won't. Not if I tell him not to.>

<You'll leave me without a host. Helpless. Blind!>

<No, Edriss. Because Marco is my son. He has the ability to see clearly from beginning to end. He inherited that trait from me.>

It was monstrous! Impossible! My own host was bargaining with me. I had expected Marco and the bandits to attack. I had not expected them to seize me, take me prisoner. They had reversed the power dynamic.

"Three . . . two . . ."

And now, I had no chance to survive. Not unless . . . unless, somehow Eva was telling the truth. Could I trust her? I knew her better than anyone ever could.

Had she seen the full picture? Would she do what she must?

"One."

"I will release your mother!" I said.

"I'll believe it when I see your nasty, slimy gray body come out of her ear," Marco said.

All lost, I told myself. *All my hopes. All my great dreams. All come down to this pathetic hope: the mercy of two humans who hate me.*

I began to disengage.

Moments later I crawled from the ear canal. I felt myself lifted up in a human hand. I saw nothing. Heard only distant rumbling. Waited for the strong human fingers to close around me, crush me, helpless as I was.

What now of all my power? I was helpless. Utterly, utterly helpless.

For a long time I waited for death.

And then, I sensed again the ear canal ahead of me. Eager, giddy, afraid, I rushed to crawl back inside her.

Yes! Yes! I was in touch with her brain. Safe! Yes, her eyes were mine, her hands, mine, her voice, mine!

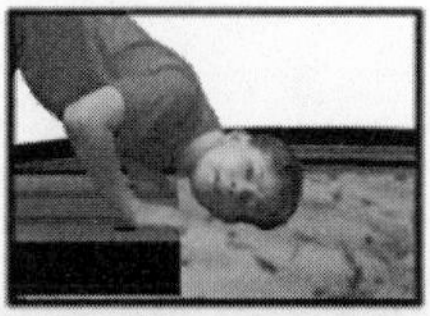

I saw tears running freely down Marco's face. The others, Andalite and beasts, looked away.

For a long time, as I rummaged frantically through Eva's most recent memories, trying to figure out what had happened, no one spoke.

And then, at long last, just as I began to access what I had missed, he nodded to the tiger.

"Sorry, Mom," he said to me. "But we have to make it look realistic."

The tiger's paw moved, withdrew, and left behind four deep, bleeding gashes in my good arm. Another too-fast-to-see movement and the Andalite slashed a shallow groove down my cheek.

"Has to look like you fought," Marco, cold, calculating Marco said as his throat choked off the words and his eyes went blind with tears.

He turned away and in a ludicrous and yet touching spectacle, the monstrous bear put a paw around his thin shoulders.

<Okay. Put her down, Ax,> the tiger said.

Fwapp!

The Andalite's tail struck and I fell.

I remained semiconscious, as often happens when a host is injured. Many Yeerks know of this strange dreamlike state. Unable to make the host body do as commanded, unable to control the mind, but still sufficiently engaged to be able to see the dreams, watch the echoes of recent events.

In this dream state I saw what had transpired. Saw my host, the boy's mother, explain to her son.

"Marco, you don't understand. If she turns up without a host, without me, they'll know something went on. They'll dig till they get the answers, Marco."

"She needs to die, Mom. You need . . . Dad and me . . . we need you back!"

Through Eva's eyes, through her memory, I saw myself, small and harmless in Marco's grip.

"I know you do, sweetheart. And, God, I need you more than life itself. But she's the one pushing for a nonviolent invasion. Visser Three wants all-out war! He wants to incinerate cities from orbit, kill and kill till we submit!"

"We'll never surrender!" Marco blazed.

Eva took his face in her hands. "Marco, that's a nice sentiment, a brave ideal. But the truth is, Marco, humans do submit. Not all, and not always, but some, maybe most. Enough will submit, Marco. Enough to give the Yeerks what they want. And the rest will be dead. Millions. Billions."

I saw Marco's hand tighten around me. I saw how close I came to that inexorable power crushing the life from me.

"You can't rely on slogans, my brave son. You have to *win* this war. For now Visser One must sur-

vive. Only she can restrain Visser Three. If she loses, or if she is seen as disloyal, he'll have his way."

Marco was not convinced. "Open war would mean humans could fight back, at least. Better to know the enemy. Know who to shoot."

"Yes, but we may well lose," Eva said. "And even if we win, how many millions or even billions of humans can we sacrifice?"

I saw his face through Eva's memory. Saw him consider. A child! And he was now deciding the fate of Earth and of the Yeerk Empire.

"Doesn't make sense," he said at last. "If open warfare would work, Visser One would support it. So, either the Yeerks have reason to believe open warfare would fail, or Visser One has some other reason for going with the slow, infiltration thing."

Clever, clever boy, I thought. *I'll enjoy the day I see the end of you. Standing there, smug, reveling in my weakness, imagining yourself invulnerable. I'll find the way to make you scream.*

"She *has* a reason," Eva said.

"Tell me."

"She has children."

CHAPTER 29

<Yeerks reproduce by fission,> the young Andalite interrupted. <They have no emotional relationship with their offspring. Indeed, Yeerks die in the act of reproducing.>

The Andalite's contempt was all too simple. But that was fine. The hatred was mutual.

"She has children by a previous human host," Eva clarified. "She has feelings for them. And, since she is no longer in command on Earth, she cannot protect them. If Visser Three launches a bloody war, they may die."

Marco was taken aback by this, though he tried to conceal it. Then he did something extraordinary. He turned to the polar bear. "Cassie?"

<I think she's telling the truth,> the bear said.

"Sorry, Mom. We can't trust anyone."

"No, you can't. But you need to know that Visser One is on trial, right now, today. On trial for her life. The decision will be up to the Council of Thirteen. They know very little about Earth. They'll

choose between Visser One and Visser Three. If they choose Visser Three they will end up following his plan, in the end."

The tiger spoke again. <We may prefer Visser Three to be in charge. He makes stupid mistakes. His people all hate and fear him, which makes his people less effective. And, we know him. Know what to expect. Visser One might be a more dangerous enemy.>

Surely that succinct summary was from an Andalite mind. It was flattering, in a way. And true, of course.

<Besides,> one of the morphed Hork-Bajir said, <Visser One knows Marco now. If she wins over Visser Three and takes back control of Earth, she kills Marco, or takes him as her own host. That way she doesn't have to worry about other Yeerks seeing his memories. She can take him herself, hunt us down one by one, and we are done for.>

<Kill Visser One now, kill Visser Three later, when we get the chance,> the second Hork-Bajir said bluntly.

Marco looked to the tiger. "What do we do, fearless leader?"

<It's your call, Marco. Your mom, your call.>

By the Kandrona itself, the tiger was human, too! Were they all humans? All but the lone Andalite?

I wanted to laugh! I wanted to run to Visser Three and spit the truth in his face: You incompetent fool, your every move has been stymied, not by highly trained Andalite guerillas, but by humans. By children!

I know now that Marco looked down at me, helpless in his hand. He closed his hand around me but did not squeeze.

"I love you, Mom," he said to Eva.

"I know, sweetheart. I love you. And I am so proud of you."

"Yeah. Dad, he . . ."

Eva shook her head. "He has to move on with his life, Marco. He thinks I'm dead. He's already grieved. And even now, the odds of my surviving are very small and remote."

At last the boy lost his composure. For a moment the self-control that made him seem so old, weakened. "You can walk away now, Mom, we can get you out of here. You could move somewhere far away, disappear. We can make it happen. We have the power. We have allies . . . friends, who have the money it would take."

Eva hugged him close, squeezing with all her might. I lay there, still, in his fist.

"We each fight this war in our own way, Marco."

Marco pulled away. He stepped back. Ran his

hand through his hair and almost seemed to beat on his own head.

"Okay. My call. Then, here's the deal. Tell Visser One when she . . . well, she'll know, won't she? So, Visser One? The deal is this: If we hear that you have retaken control of Yeerk forces on Earth, we drop the dime on you. We contact Visser Three, the Council directly even, and we tell them how you reached out to us. We've recorded this little meeting. The recording goes to your bosses, and that'll be it for you. Other than that, this whole thing never happened. That's the deal. You don't know us, we don't know you, we were never here."

A recording? How? I looked around, searching for a recording device. Futile, of course. We were behind a hologram. With a hologram emitter this sophisticated anything could be hidden.

"And by the way?" Marco added. "If you get to thinking we can't contact the Council of Thirteen, guess again. Not all your fellow Yeerks are loyal."

He held out his hand, reluctance making him tremble. "Not this time, Yeerk," he said to me. "You don't die today. But someday."

He gave me back to Eva. That's when I discovered how my fate was decided.

CHAPTER 30

I lay still with my host unconscious. I could not see with her eyes or hear with her ears. I lay there, alone with only my own memory now.

The "bandits" had presumably withdrawn. They had presumably turned off the hologram that concealed us. Soon someone would discover me. I could only hope it would not be a Taxxon. A Taxxon's loyalty and self-restraint were very doubtful when there was fresh meat to be had without a struggle.

I lay, helpless, waiting for the swelling in Eva's brain to go down, for function to return. Waited, and remembered the story I had not told the Council.

I had lied to them. Of course, I had lied.

Essam and I knew the Kandrona was running down. Starvation lay ahead. Essam said he would die rather than contact the Empire.

Not me. I wasn't ready to die. I loved life as a human. Loved my life as Allison Kim, as Hildy's wife, as a mother.

I had gone over. I was as much human as Yeerk. But how to survive? And more important, how to rule? Because as much as I enjoyed my life on Earth, I still burned with ambition to be a visser, to command and control the only Class-Five species we knew.

I simply wanted to shape the invasion of Earth to allow me to maintain control over the tactics and the strategy. We could enslave the people of Earth gradually. They would never need to know that we were there among them. Until we *were* them, and they us, and all under my power.

I could do it all, if only I could present the Empire with a *fait accompli,* an accomplished fact.

So I began work at a feverish pace. We moved to a more typical American community, a midsized city on one of the oceans. There I used my superior computer skills to steal millions of dollars from bank accounts. I formed fake companies and raised millions more from the sale of stock.

And, once I had the seed money, several hundred million, I began to create The Sharing.

It would cater to one of the most fundamental human weaknesses: the need to belong. The fear of loneliness. The hunger to be special. The craving for an exaggerated importance.

I would make a haven for the weak, the inadequate, the fearful. I would wrap it up in all the bright packaging that humans love so much.

The Sharing would never be about weak people being led to submit to a stronger will, no, no, it would be about family, virtue, righteousness, brotherhood and sisterhood. I would offer people an identity. A place to go. I would give them a new vision of themselves as part of something larger, erasing their individuality.

I needed only one thing before I could go to the Empire, call the Council of Thirteen, and present them with my accomplished fact: I needed one human, just one, to submit voluntarily.

If I could show them one human who had surrendered his or her will and freedom, without threat of violence, I could convince the Empire to follow my path. The way of infiltration.

The first meeting of The Sharing took place on a Saturday. Thirty-five people attended.

I had done a tremendous job in a very short time. I had studied human history, supplementing what Allison Kim already knew. I studied every cult, every movement, every great, mesmerizing leader that had ever held sway over humans.

And by the time those thirty-five humans came into the rented hall, I had adorned the walls with symbols and flags and icons. All the visual nonsense that moves the susceptible human mind.

They filed in, some in small groups, but most alone. They were stirred by the inspirational music. Flattered by the attention paid them by attendants I'd hired from a temp agency. Impressed by the expensively produced booklets we handed out. Awed by the pictures and symbols that draped the walls.

I spoke to them from the stage. Not as Allison Kim, of course, because all my links to Allison Kim would have to be concealed before my fellow Yeerks arrived.

I had carefully picked a human host for just this one purpose. His name was Lawrence Alter. A real estate salesman. I changed his name to Lore David Altman. Three name combinations were popular then.

He was a charismatic man with a loud, deep voice and an abundance of hair. Just the sort of face that humans respond to, though his brain was a wasteland compared to Allison's.

Allison Kim had been left handcuffed to a radiator in a hotel room, awaiting my return.

Later, after it was over, I found I couldn't recall exactly what I'd said to this first meeting of The Sharing, not the specific words. A lot of high-flown rhetoric touching on the themes humans love to hear: that they are special, superior, a chosen few. That their failures in life are all someone else's fault.

That mystical, unseen forces and secret knowledge will give them power.

The next Saturday there were more than twice the number of humans. And already I had begun to explain that there was an "Outer" Sharing, and an "Inner" one. The humans in the "Outer" Sharing were wiser, better, more moral, superior to the average human, but not as superior as those lucky few who had entered the "Inner" Sharing.

Of course at that point there was no "Inner" Sharing. Just seventy or eighty humans sitting in plush chairs and being fed an endless diet of words that had no clear meaning.

The Inner-Sharing, that was the test of true greatness. And all a human had to do to enter was to surrender their will.

This was what Essam, who had infested only Lowenstein and Hildy, would not credit: that humans would surrender their freedom in exchange for empty words. But I had infested the lost soldier, and the even more lost Jenny Lines. I had tasted human defeat and superstition and weakness.

I knew.

CHAPTER 31

It was so easy. Disturbingly easy. I had been in a human host for a long time, gone from the negligible Jenny Lines to the formidable Allison Kim. I had come to have some sympathy for humans, even as I plotted their destruction as a race.

I had, or felt I had, human children of my own.

And so, a part of me, a small part of me was like Essam and did not want to believe that humans could be this easily fooled. Part of me, a small part, was disappointed that I was right.

The first was named Rich Huntley. He almost begged me to let him join the Inner-Sharing.

"Why?" I asked him. "Why do you want to join?"

"Because I really believe in all the things you're saying."

"You can believe without being in the Inner-Sharing," I said. "Why is it so important to you?"

It took a while, but in the end he told the truth.

"Because I want to be part of something. Something big and important."

Part of something. Anything, so long as he could be a *part*, and not be himself alone.

"If you join the Inner-Sharing it will mean losing all your individual will," I said.

He shrugged.

"It will mean that you will never again be free of The Sharing."

"I don't want to be free of it! I love The Sharing. I love you, Brother Lore!"

"You will be apart, different."

"Yeah! That's what I want!"

He was so willing, so eager, I suspected some sort of clever trap. It couldn't be this easy. Humans could not surrender their own individuality for nothing but a promise that they would be "special." It was insane!

One, final test.

Essam had left his host, agreeing to help me with this experiment. Poor Essam, he thought he would win the bet.

I raised Essam from a small jar half-filled with water. I held him in my hand. I knew how we looked to humans. Slugs. Worms. Leeches. The reference points were never flattering.

The human, Rich Huntley, recoiled. The sight of

Essam in his natural state sickened his human sensibilities.

"Rich," I said, "this is a Yeerk. To become a member of the Inner-Sharing, you must allow me to put him in your ear. He will enter your brain. He will take over your life."

He was nervous, afraid. "But then I'm in, right? Then I'm in the Inner-Sharing, right?"

"Right."

"Does it . . . does it hurt?"

"No."

"Okay. Okay, then. Yeah. Let's do it. Let's do it."

We did it. Essam found himself looking out through Huntley's eyes at me.

"You win, Sub-Visser," he said.

I was generous in victory. "We win, Essam. All Yeerks win."

"And humans lose."

"The first law of evolution, Essam: survival of the most fit. And it's not as if we intend to eat them," I joked. "We're not predators. We are parasites. They'll live. They'll be fed and be cared for."

"They'll be slaves."

"Look around that mind while you're in there, Essam. What else was this human good for?"

Essam left the host and we disposed of the human.

We recorded the entire thing. Proof to the Empire that I had not only located a true Class-Five species, but that we could begin harvesting human hosts right away, without the loss of so much as a single Hork-Bajir.

I contacted the Empire.

Essam knew I had contacted the Empire. And he agreed. That was not the point where Essam and I parted ways. I misled the Council on that. I couldn't tell them that I had every intention at first of keeping the children.

The rupture between Essam and me came weeks later, when it became increasingly clear to me that I no longer had any use for Allison Kim. I needed to spend all my time now as Lore David Altman, spiritual guide of The Sharing.

"What will you do with Allison?" Essam asked.

"What do you mean, what will I do? We will have to kill her and destroy the body. And while we're at it, we'll need to erase Hildy Gervais, as well. Hildy is tied to Allison and it will be better if it seems that both have simply moved away."

"You would kill the mother and father of these children?"

"Essam, we have no choice. Our new hosts will simply adopt the orphaned children. They're young. The children will be fine!"

"Yes. As you say, Sub-Visser."

"Soon there will be no 'sub,'" I said happily. "I

will be Visser. And a visser in the single digits, Essam. What can they deny me, now? I could be Visser Six. Or three. I could even be Visser One, Essam. Won't that be wonderful? Visser One!"

I was too caught up in my own visions of power to spot the warning signs.

The rest of what I'd told the Council was true. Or mostly true: Essam had overpowered me, starved me till I left Allison Kim. He'd left me with access to Lore David Altman.

I did go in search of Essam. But not to kill him.

He had my children. I wanted them back.

I still wanted them back.

"Visser One! Visser One!"

"Mmmm?"

"Wake up. You have been given a stimulant that will bring you back to full alertness."

A human-Controller leaned over me. I was on my back, on a table, in what might have been a hospital room. But I knew it was just a part of the pool facility.

<Is she awake?> Visser Three demanded.

"Yes, Visser. I have repaired the most recent injuries. She seems to have been slashed by a large animal, probably a member of the cat family, and by—"

<Get her to the trial chamber. Now.>

Visser Three's large Andalite eyes hovered above me. The rage was a banked fire, for now. The fear was fresh and bright.

<The Council demands our presence, Visser One,> he said dully.

I rose, groggy, woozy from blood loss, from injuries old and new, from the aftereffects of unconsciousness.

We walked toward the chamber. The guards walked with us. As before. But with one difference. It was clear now that we were *both* being watched.

CHAPTER 32

I sat. Visser Three stood. The Hork-Bajir guard had been doubled. Outside the chamber the Hork-Bajir were multiplying, rushing to obey Garoff's direct orders. Orders that might result in Visser Three's arrest. But would more likely result in his immediate execution.

After all, a morph-capable warrior is very, very hard to hold on to.

I should have been pleased to see him brought low. But I was not. I, too, was now sure to be condemned. And I would not have the advantage of a quick, painless death.

<You're a thief, a slave mistress, a murderer many times over,> Eva said. <How is it I can feel even the slightest pity for you?>

The Council appeared in the hologram. I searched those hooded faces for some clue. Were they drawn slightly apart, those corrupt, powerful old Yeerks? Was there a tension there? Or was I merely desperate?

Garoff spoke, his voice grave. "There are a few questions left to be cleared up, Visser One. How did the children escape? How did Essam die, and how did his host, Hildy, survive?"

"You . . . you want me to continue my story?"

"Don't make the mistake of believing you are still on trial, Visser One. The trial is over. We have already decided on a verdict." He looked deliberately at Visser Three and added, "Two verdicts."

Strange. Much as we hated each other, Visser Three and I were together in the same boat, as the human expression goes. A boat that was heading for the rocks of a lee shore.

<I enjoyed it when you sailed. Before I realized it was all a setup to explain your disappearance.>

<It wasn't all a setup, human. I miss it.>

"Tell us, in succinct fashion, what happened after Essam left with your progeny."

"Yes, Council member."

I tried to turn my memory back to the hectic days, days of such soaring hope mingled with such bitter loss. But I kept seeing a billowing white sail above me; feeling salt spray on my face, stinging my eyes; my hand on the tiller, the pressure of it against my palm; the sense that the boat itself was alive, endowed with life by the need of sky and sea to create some sort of union.

Eva's husband, my second husband, so to speak,

was there, lying back, feet propped, a drink in one hand, a book he wasn't reading in the other hand. And Marco, of course, climbing dangerously in the rigging, playing superhero.

I had shielded myself from the boy and his father. I had learned by then not to let human emotion affect me. I was an actor, playing a part to perfection. I used Eva's mind, her instincts, to be a good wife and a good mother, even as I plotted and waited and plotted some more.

I never let Eva see my children. Never let her know. I watched them through other hosts, but not through her eyes. She hated me so for what I was doing to her family, her son. Somehow I never could stand the possibility of her knowing that I, too, had children.

We do what we have to do in life. Human or Yeerk. Morality is an illusion, a shield for the weak. It is all about the hunger for power. I knew that. Believed that.

And yet, I could not let my host see that I was a mother, too. I could stand her hatred. I could not stand the insinuating pity, the appeals to a shared love.

"We're waiting," Garoff said testily.

"Yes. Yes," I said. "Hildy. Essam. It was . . . it . . ." I shook my head and received a jolt of pain from my twisted bones.

"I went after them," I said. "I chased them. It was not easy. Essam was no fool. Allison was surely no fool. And Hildy had lived an interesting life. He knew the places a human could hide. Nevertheless, I found them.

"The twins were sick. Both with high fevers. Allison and Essam took them to a doctor. The doctor admitted them to a hospital, and their names popped up in a computer search.

"I was there very quickly. Three days had passed. I knew Essam would be starving. I hoped to use the presence of the Kandrona to torture him. Starvation is so much more painful when salvation is near."

<You were going to save him.>

<No. No, human, I was not. He had abandoned me. Spurned me. After all we . . .>

<Jealousy?>

<Jealousy? Don't be idiotic. Not jealousy, rage, rage! How could they? Essam? Allison? He had a duty to me. And she, hadn't I treated her kindly? And yet, she tricked me, used me, and then turned on me!>

<My God, do you hear yourself? You use and enslave and kill without mercy and you expect loyalty?>

"Visser One, if you are having some sort of difficulty in focusing . . ."

"No, Council Member Garoff. I'm fine." I drew a

deep breath and steeled myself, hoping at best to get through to the end of the proceeding with some dignity.

I found Essam starving. Hildy, never the most emotionally stable of humans, was cracking under the strain of experiencing Essam's pain. I am told it's very difficult for a host to endure the death of a Yeerk.

I approached Essam, took him by surprise in a stairwell of the hospital. He attacked me. But I was armed.

"Go ahead, kill me! I'm already dead!" he cried.

"Why are the twins here?"

"What? Do you actually pretend to care?" he mocked. "They have a virus, a resistant strain of some sort. If I had the ship, if I had access to the ship's computer, I could synthesize an antiviral. I could . . . I . . . ."

He staggered. He'd lost control of his host for a moment. He was weakening swiftly.

"You betrayed me and you betrayed your race," I said.

"Your race is sick! Sick and twisted and evil!" It was Hildy talking, on his own, uncontrolled.

"We are parasites, Mr. Gervais," I said. "You're a predator. Go ask a cow or a pig what they think of humans. We do what we are born to do."

"I'm dying." Essam again. "Dying. Don't . . . don't hurt the kids. You can't . . ."

He collapsed suddenly, utterly. It was as if every tendon in his body had been cut at the same moment. He lay there, breathing but little else. I reached down and turned his head. Left ear. Right ear. Essam was trying to emerge from the right ear. He was halfway out, escaping the host in the moment of death, as instinct tells us to do.

I grabbed him and pulled him the rest of the way. But he was still more attached than I'd thought. I suppose death had already reached part of his body. I held half a Yeerk in my hand. He moved very little, then he stopped moving altogether.

I put him into my pocket. A strange moment. A moment I'll never forget. So small, we Yeerks, compared with the host bodies we take. So small I could stick my friend in my pocket.

I was alone on Earth. The only Yeerk. It would take weeks for anyone else to arrive. Maybe months.

I was more lonely than ever.

Hildy woke, slowly. But he was not the same human. Bits of Essam still stuck to his brain. Dead nerve endings were tied into his. Some of his neurons fired through dead Yeerk tissue.

He tried to attack me. Pushed me out of the stair-

well, into a corridor. He tried to choke me with his bare hands. Allison saw us fighting. Nurses and interns and security guards were running to intervene.

They pulled Hildy off me. They dragged him away, raving about aliens. They held him for psychiatric observation.

As soon as I could get free, I went after Allison. She was gone. The twins were still there. Allison had had no choice but to leave them, of course. She was afraid I'd kill her, or infest her again.

I knew she would come back for the children. I relied on it. She was very clever. She came back disguised as a doctor. A wig, colored contact lenses, so on. But I knew her too well.

I killed her.

<My God. How could you do it? How could you do such an evil thing?>

<No choice. If she lived, she'd have come after me. She was respected, believable. She was dangerous. She knew I was Lore David Altman. She knew how to find me.>

Garoff nodded. "You eliminated this troublesome host."

"Yes."

"And the human Hildy? Obviously you did not kill him."

"The humans diagnosed him as mad. He could rave all he liked, it wouldn't matter. No one would ever believe him."

"And the children?" Garoff asked.

"I left them where they were. In the hospital. In time they were judged to be abandoned and put up for adoption. That is where human pair-bonded couples take over care of another human couple's progeny."

"And then?"

I took a deep breath. It was all at an end, now. "I waited for the first ships to arrive and I built The Sharing. Once the first Yeerks arrived I began to work feverishly to acquire willing hosts. Once we had enough willing hosts we would have the forces necessary to begin taking involuntary hosts as well.

"A few, then a dozen, then a hundred. We built our financial base and began the secret construction of this very facility: the first great Yeerk pool on planet Earth.

"Finally, when I judged the time was right, I eliminated Lore David Altman. Humans will tear down a living leader but revere a dead one. I left behind sufficient writings . . . vague nostrums, platitudes, absurdities, prophecies, the sorts of transparent nonsense that humans pore over endlessly.

"The time was right for me to change hosts. I found this body. I took it. And I continued running

The Sharing from behind the scenes, building facilities, creating false fronts, infiltrating, swelling our numbers, all with never a Dracon beam fired."

I smiled, amused by my own persistent pride. I had done great things.

<You're a murderer, Yeerk. That soldier, Jenny, Lowenstein, Allison, Lore . . .>

<And you would have had your day, human, when the time came that I tired of you.>

"Is that everything, Visser One?" Garoff asked.

Everything, I thought. *Everything but the years of missing Essam, missing Allison. Regrets. Rage. The thrill of seeing my power grow as my plan came to fruition. The impotent despair of watching my children from afar. Half Yeerk, half almost human.*

I had taken this final host because, at least unconsciously, I wanted to know the life I could never really know. The love of a spouse, an equal. The love of a child.

But none of it had ever really touched me. I'd had my fling with humanity. I was Yeerk once more. I was Visser One.

"It's enough," I said.

"Then the Council will make known its judgments."

CHAPTER 33

We were kept waiting a while, Visser Three and I. A long while, despite Garoff's earlier claim that judgment had already been rendered.

We did not speak.

I sat there, broken in body, friendless, defeated, with no company but the voice of my host. She was sickened by her own temporary compromise with me.

<I shouldn't have helped you,> she said. <Even if it did lead to open war, I shouldn't have helped you. You filthy, evil thing. I thought I'd found something decent inside you. I thought you were a mother, too.>

<I was. I am.>

<At least now you'll die and I'll be free.>

I laughed. <You'll die, too, human. What freedom is there in death?>

<I'll be free of you.>

The wait stretched on. On and on. I was fed.

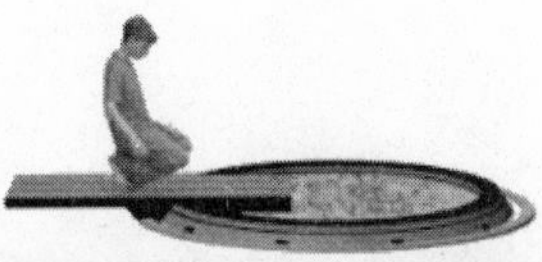

Visser Three was allowed to feed. There were Dracon beams trained on us every second of the time.

At last the hologram glowed again. The scene had changed. It took me a moment to notice it, but it had changed: One of the Taxxons was gone, and one of the Hork-Bajir as well. The Council of Thirteen was, as far as I could see, the Council of Eleven. Visser Three's stalk eyes swiveled to see my reaction. I nodded slightly. Yes, there had been quite a debate among the Council members.

But Garoff was still there.

"Vissers One and Three, you have jointly or individually committed a dozen death penalty offenses. Visser Three, you lied to and manipulated this Council. Visser One, you clearly committed numerous death penalty offenses during a period early in your invasion of Earth. You are both condemned to death by Kandrona starvation."

I felt nothing. It was what I had known must happen. Death. The most terrible death we know.

"Both sentences suspended."

Neither of us moved. The words meant nothing. What? Sentences suspended? What did that mean?

The tiniest flicker of hope . . .

"Visser Three, you have failed to make progress with Earth. Your sentence is suspended for now because we simply have no one ready to take over operations there. Earth is vital. If you want the suspension to become permanent, give us Earth!"

Garoff clenched his Hork-Bajir fist. "We need hosts. We need them badly. The Andalites are building up their forces."

Visser Three was suddenly bursting with energy. <Yes, Council Members, yes! I will give you Earth. I will begin the annihilation of their cities as soon —>

"No, Visser, you will not. The Andalites have at long last become fully aware of the situation on Earth. They are assembling a massive fleet in orbit around their home world. It will be ready to launch within months. Target: Uncertain."

<Not Earth?>

"Earth. Or, the Anati world. It will depend on which they decide is more important. But, as you know, Visser Three, the Andalites are slow to commit. A sudden, violent war on Earth would be sure to draw them in. Do you have the forces to fight a full Andalite fleet containing thirty of their Dome ships, Visser Three?"

Visser Three chose not to respond rather than admit that half that many Dome ships could wipe his forces out within minutes of emerging from Z-space.

"No, I didn't think so," Garoff said dryly. "Visser One, we wish the Andalites to attack us in the Anati

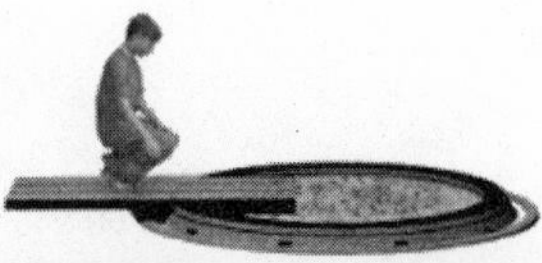

system. But not immediately. The planet in question is ringed by numerous moons and large asteroids that will allow us to place Dracon cannon. Cannon are easier to come by than ships."

"I . . . I don't understand," I said. "Do you . . . are you ordering me . . ."

"You are too valuable to dispose of just yet. You remain the most successful military officer in the Empire, despite your illegal and troubling methods. You are ordered to proceed immediately to the Anati system and take over the subjugation of her sentient race or races, and prepare to resist an Andalite attack. Succeed, and you will live. Fail, and —"

Eva's attack was sudden, wild, and unexpected.

"NO!" she cried with her own mouth. "NOOOO! Kill her! Kill her! You have to —"

I clamped down hard on the speech centers and stifled her words.

<No! No! No! No!>

"What's the matter, human? Sick of my company? Ah hah hah hah! A new planet! A chance to redeem everything!"

Garoff shot me a distasteful look. A look a human might reserve for someone who had belched loudly in a restaurant.

". . . as I was saying, fail us, Visser One, and the sentence of death will be carried out. That is the decision of the Council."

The hologram was gone.

<No! Let me go. Kill me, but get out of my head!>

I closed my eyes, held them shut, then opened them again on a whole new world. A whole new world of hope!

A new planet! A new race! No more troubling humans. And this time, this time, I would do it right.

The children? Visser Three had made Darwin a host. Darwin, my son, was lost to me. But what about Madra? Was she still free? Could I . . .

No. I couldn't. Not yet. Someday, not yet.

But someday she would know me. I would tell her all about me, all about who I was, how she had come to exist. And she would love me, as a daughter loves a mother.

And if not, then I could always infest Madra, place some well-trained Yeerk in her head. Then she would love me. She'd have no choice.

Yes, it was all going to work out fine. It was a great, big, lovely galaxy of opportunity.

"Well, Visser Three, nice try," I said jovially. "I thought you had me there, for a while. I thought at long last you had me."

<Oh, but I did, Visser One. It was the Andalite bandits who saved you. If they hadn't attacked . . .> He smiled an Andalite smile. <One more reason to exterminate them.>

"Yes. Well, about those Andalite bandits, since we're past all this unpleasantness between us, I guess I could tell you . . ."

<What could you tell me?>

"Oh, nothing. Nothing at all, Visser. Not a thing."